BRAC
7/2020

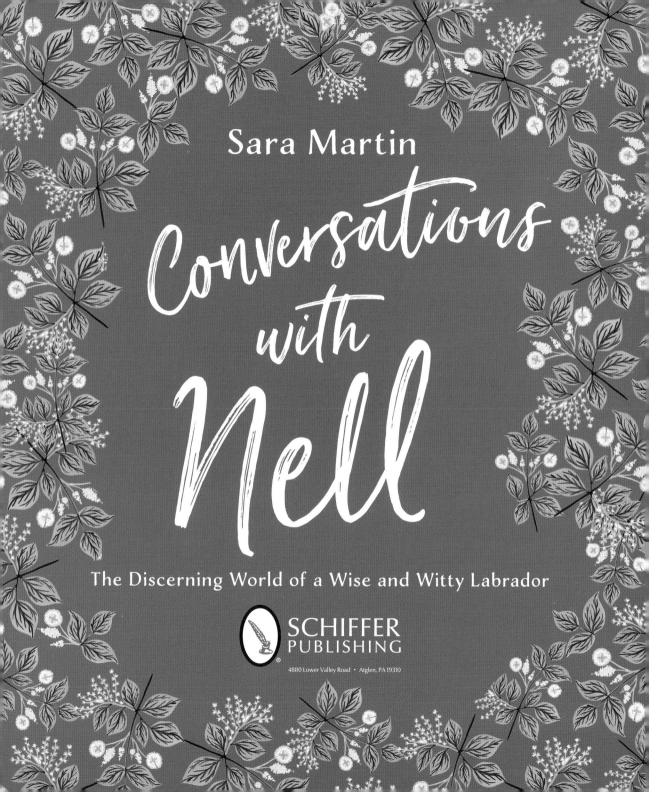

Sara Martin

Conversations with Nell

The Discerning World of a Wise and Witty Labrador

SCHIFFER
PUBLISHING

4880 Lower Valley Road • Atglen, PA 19310

Notes from Nell's Fan Club

Cheerful and brilliant and funny. If my dream ever comes true and I make it to England, forget Big Ben. I'm looking for Nell.

—*Amanda, Illinois, USA*

If you want to appeal to your inner puppy, read this. A must for dog lovers who have no problem with humanizing animals. WARNING . . . highly addictive reading.

—*Kath James-Carroll from Yorkshire, UK*

Anyone who has a dog, loves dogs, could not fail to be enthralled by Nell and her family. It's like being a fly (or flea!!) on the wall. You just want to scratch and scratch until you get the next crazy update on happenings in Nell's household. Absolutely love it!

— *Elizabeth Whibley, Warwickshire, UK*

Simply outstanding! Sara's writing is superb, witty, charming, utterly believable . . . so much so that if I EVER heard that Nell and the others don't actually speak, I would be damaged for life . . . ADORE THEM ALL and am beside myself with excitement at the prospect of, at long last, THE BOOK! HURRAH!

—*Joy Wood, Somerset, UK*

I love conversations with Nell. Cheers me up every day, and I look forward to the "life lessons of a Labrador." I actually read them out to my two Labradors. Keep up the good work!

—*Claire, Glasgow*

Nell kills me!! SHE is my (s)hero. So subtle, so collected, so very funny! I always look forward to reading these. Please keep them coming.

—*Dee Blue, Sudan, Africa*

An even bigger laugh than yesterday . . . one of the best . . . just in communication with a thread that wanted to know our favourite books as children (and that's a long way back for me) . . . however, I think yours when it comes out would be a favourite with young and old (excluding the tinies, I think, who wouldn't get all those clever names) . . . and today's should be in it. It will be interesting to know who does the illustrations . . . plus photos of course . . . or perhaps just the photos and our imaginations doing the rest . . . we need to get back to using our imaginations. Mm . . . a lot of work for you because it is all brilliant . . . and fresh.

— *Winifred Stanton, Bristol, UK*

The exciting adventures and daily escapades of the ever-growing Martin family make me wish I could join this fun and fabulous family!

—*Susan Haraway, Texas, USA*

In 2015, I moved back in with my parents, who have Alzheimer's/dementia. I also, have 2 sons, in their 20s. Oldest is sometimes childlike. He was diagnosed ADHD. Beginning to think he's possibly autistic. Youngest is going into the military, if all goes well, in two to three weeks. Plus, I work third shift in retail as a stocker.

Sometimes when I feel like Life has thrown more at me than I can handle, I'm feeling overwhelmed, along with the other 101 things I'm feeling, your *Conversations with Nell* show up on my timeline. I read them, my morning gets better, and back off I go to whatever I was doing. Thanks for making my mornings, days, nights, and in between enjoyable!

—*Connie Lynn Wright, Kentucky, USA*

Nell, you just R.O.C.K! There is no higher compliment I can think of giving.

—*Dilesh Perera, Singapore*

Humorous narratives lead the reader into this amazing and curious world of Nell and her housemates. Allowing personalities and individualities gives the reader permission to accept differences in themselves and others.

—*Amy Stapay, Seattle, WA, USA*

Copyright © 2020 by Sara Martin

Library of Congress Control Number: 2019947418

Cover and interior design by Ashley Millhouse
Type set in Adorn Roman/Chronicle Text G1

ISBN: 978-0-7643-5929-3
Printed in China

Published by Schiffer Publishing, Ltd.
4880 Lower Valley Road
Atglen, PA 19310
Phone: (610) 593-1777; Fax: (610) 593-2002
E-mail: Info@schifferbooks.com
Web: www.schifferbooks.com

For our complete selection of fine books on this and related subjects, please visit our website at www.schifferbooks.com. You may also write for a free catalog.

Schiffer Publishing's titles are available at special discounts for bulk purchases for sales promotions or premiums. Special editions, including personalized covers, corporate imprints, and excerpts, can be created in large quantities for special needs. For more information, contact the publisher.

We are always looking for people to write books on new and related subjects. If you have an idea for a book, please contact us at proposals@schifferbooks.com.

Other Schiffer Books on Related Subjects:

Senior Dogs Across America
by Nancy LeVine

ISBN 978-0-7643-5111-2

**Baking for Dogs: The Best Recipes
from Dog's Deli**

by Friederike Friedel. With photographs by
Thomas Schultze,

ISBN 978-0-7643-3248-7

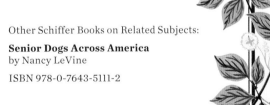

⊰ TABLE OF CONTENTS ⊱

TABLE OF CONTENTS

❧ DEDICATION ❦

Nell: This book is dedicated to your lovely mother, Sally.

Me: Yes, it is. She always loved my stories.

Nell: I know you think about her every day and miss her very much.

Me: Yes.

Nell: So remember what I told you about the Guardians. When we lose the ones we love, they have not really gone. They become our Guardians and they watch over us.

Me: Yes.

Nell: So when things happen to make you smile, like the sun coming out on a cloudy day, or the smile of a stranger when you are feeling low, then know she is there.

Me: Yes.

Nell: She and I talked about this after we lost little Monty. Just before she became ill.

Me: Yes, you did. He was a lovely dog.

Nell: Yes. And she agreed that becoming a Guardian was a wonderful thing. She said when her time came, she would be honoured to watch over you all, and that is exactly what she is doing.

Me: But we didn't know we would lose her so soon, Nell.

Nell: I know.

Me: Yes. Sorry.

Nell: No need to be sorry.

Cast of Characters

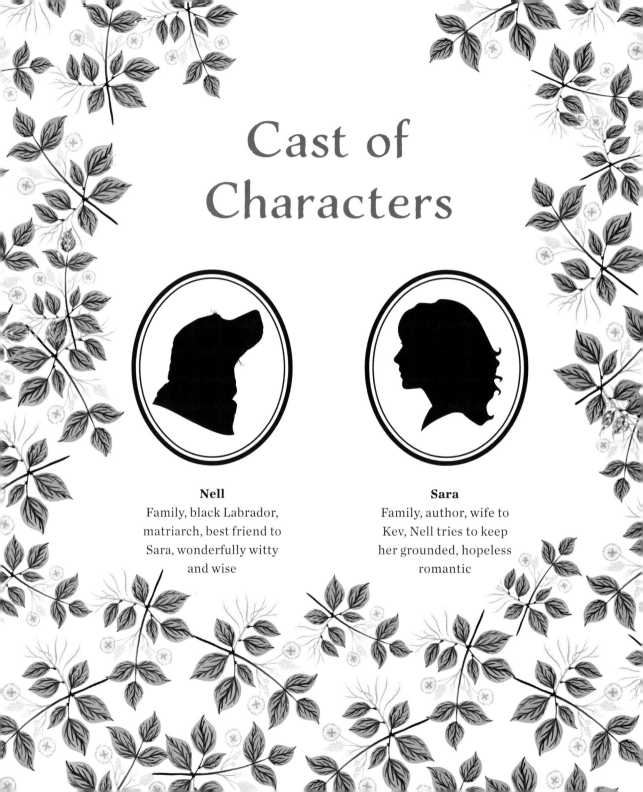

Nell
Family, black Labrador, matriarch, best friend to Sara, wonderfully witty and wise

Sara
Family, author, wife to Kev, Nell tries to keep her grounded, hopeless romantic

Dave
Family, big black Labrador,
brother to Harriet,
nephew to Nell

Mutley
Family, elderly Patterdale
terrier, grandfather,
entrepreneur

Poppy
Family, Maltese/Yorkshire
terrier cross, amazing chef
(just try her scones)

Gladys
Family, black Pomeranian,
dancer, sleeps in
Nell's handbag

Harriet
Family, chocolate
Labrador, sister to Dave,
niece to Nell

Kev
Family, husband to Sara,
can do no wrong in
Nell's eyes

The Cat
Family, a strawberry
blonde cat, adores sequins,
dressmaking, decorating,
and Dave, a little theatrical

HUMAN CHARACTERS

Alexandra: Sister to Sara

Alex: Vet

Alice: Family, daughter, mother to Jonathan Sky and Faye Raine, lives near Berlin

Charlotte: Sister to Sara

Chris: Family, son, lives in Toronto

Dudley: Resides at the Haunted Hotel

Emily: Vet

Faye Raine: Family, daughter to Alice, granddaughter, lives near Berlin, born May 2019

James: Chauffeur

Jonathan Sky: Family, son to Alice, grandson, lives near Berlin, but visits (thank goodness)

Richard: Vet

Sally: Family, Sara's late mother; this book is dedicated to her

Sarah: Owner of Cottage Hotel

Scarlett: Niece to Sara and Kev, daughter to Charlotte, gave Dave his name

Tom: Vet

Tony: Postman, best friend to Dave, lead singer of the "Old Gaffers" sea shanty crew

William: Owner of Cottage Hotel

MISCELLANEOUS CHARACTERS

The Beefies: An evil gang of seagulls

Count Bingo Flamingo: A greater flamingo, head of the Flamingo Foreign Legion, French

Malcolm: Family, a polite flamingo

Marwood: Sloth

Sid the Fish: Otter, fishmonger

Stephen Seagull: Seagull, head of the evil seagull gang the Beefies, nasty piece of work

Timothy: Family, turkey, rescued by Nell

CANINE CHARACTERS

Charlie Shepherd / Siegfried Schäferhund: German shepherd, love of Nell's life, secret agent

Dartmouth Dachshunds: Dachshunds from Dartmouth in Devon, always willing to get involved

Dorothy: Red setter, friend of Nell's, one of the Salcombe setters

Ernest: An elderly Jack Russell, friend of Mutley's, spectacles, smokes a pipe

Fluffy: Black Labrador puppy, Dave and Harriet's sister, lives in Oxfordshire

Frenchies: French bulldogs, love dancing

John the Doberman: Poppy's fiance and owner of Starbarks at Kingsbridge quay

Michael Bouvier: A Bouvier des Flandres, Canadian, famous singer

Monty: Family, much missed Yorkshire terrier

Richard Price: Black Russian terrier

Rita Pawreno: Chihuahua, dancer

Robert: Rotweiler, bodyguard to Mutley

Ron Gilbert: Great Dane from Torquay, practical handy dog

Sally: Golden retriever, in love with Dave, works with Charlie, beautiful

Seamus: Terrier of mixed origins, living with Charlotte

Valerie: French bulldog

Vivian: Irish leopard, deaf

Welsh corgis: Corgis, they love to sing and knit, beautiful voices

Map of Devon

WHERE WE LIVE

Me: We live in the beautiful county of Devon in the South West of the UK. Kev drew this map to show the places we like to visit.

Nell: It is an Area of Outstanding Natural Beauty and we are extremely fortunate to live so near to the sea.

Me: Yes. Our cottage is on a farm and The Cat lives in the Big House just nearby.

Nell: Dartmoor National Park is to the North of us.

Me: And so is Totnes where you can catch a train to London and beyond.

Nell: Which you do regularly without me I might add.

Me: Not that regularly. To the North East is Torquay, a seaside town on the English Riviera.

Nell: Then there is Dartmouth, a beautiful coastal town with delightful dachshunds and an excellent Barks and Spencer.

Me: Salcombe is favoured by the yachting crowd and full of boats.

Nell: Kingsbridge is our local town with more boats, a quay and far too many Beefies for my liking.

Me: Hope Cove is home to the Cottage Hotel and the most beautiful views in Devon.

Nell: The closest beach to us is Bantham a lovely place to surf and swim.

Me: Thurlestone Hotel and the Beachhouse at South Milton are favourite places to eat and Kev has added Meadow Walk and Tony the Postman's van.

Nell: As well as an awful lot of sheep and cows.

Me: We mustn't forget the Secret Beach.

Nell: Which must remain secret. So, stop right there. You have said quite enough.

Me: Yes. Sorry.

Introduction

ᚼ INTRODUCTION ᚼ

Nell: This is where we introduce ourselves.

Me: I don't think that's necessary, Nell, I've known you since you were a puppy.

Nell: Good grief. I mean introduce ourselves to our readers. Not everyone knows who we are. They don't all follow your blog you know. Do keep up.

Me: Of course. My name is Sara and I live in a cottage near the sea in the beautiful South Hams in Devon, United Kingdom with my husband Kev and our five dogs.

Nell: I am Nell, a pedigree black Labrador and head of the family.

Me: I'm not sure you can say that, Nell.

Nell: I just did.

Me: Yes, but Kev and I are your owners.

Nell: If that's what you think then it's fine with me. We dogs know the real truth.

Me: The eldest of our dogs is a rescue Patterdale called Mutley. He toured the United States for many years with his swing band but has settled down now and is concentrating on his various enterprises such as Pizza Mutt and Walbarks.

Nell: Yes, Mutley is quite the entrepreneur and known in the East End of London as the Dogfather.

Me: After Nell there is Poppy, a Maltese/Yorkshire terrier cross.

Nell: Poppy is a wonderful chef. Her scones are renowned. She flies helicopters in her spare time.

Me: Poppy also likes to carry a sword. Just in case. She's engaged to John the Doberman who runs the local Starbarks. Am I saying too much again? Sorry.

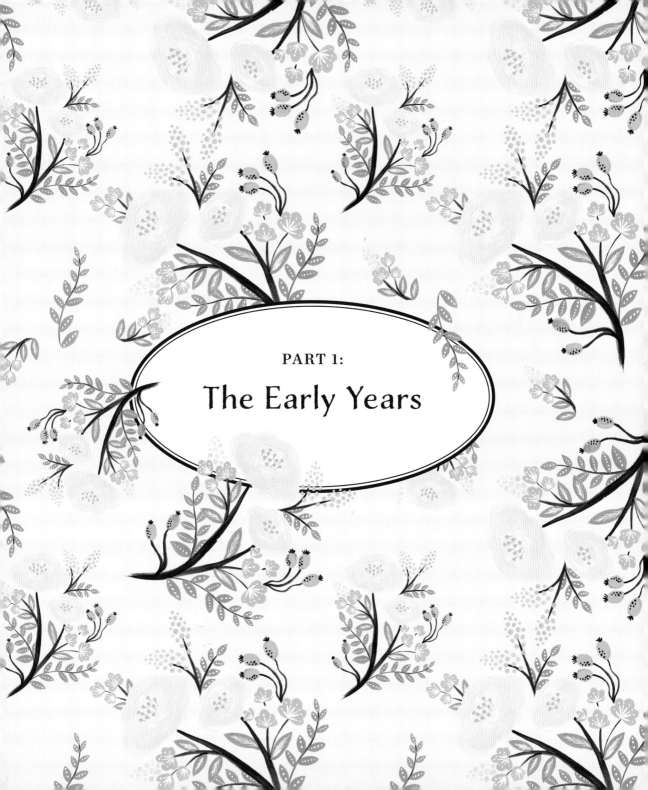

PART 1:

The Early Years

CHAPTER 1:

Dave

Nell: Who is that?

Me: Well, you know I have been a bit down?

Nell: Yes, we discussed the situation and I was kind.

Me: You were.

Nell: I'm still waiting to know about that strange animal.

Me: He's not a strange animal Nell. He's a baby Labrador.

Nell: With mud on his head.

Me: He had Weetabix on his head the time before.

Nell: What do you mean "the time before"?

Me: I've visited him a few times.

Nell: What?

Me: At the stables where you were born.

Nell: What?

Me: He's your nephew.
Your sister Maisie is his mother.

Nell: Ah, just a family visit then.

Me: Sort of.

Nell: There is more?

Me: He's called Dave.

Nell: That's a ridiculous name. What was Maisie thinking?

Me: Actually, my niece Scarlett named him. I like it.

Nell: Go on. There's more. I can tell.

Me: The thing is...

Nell: Spit it out for goodness sake.

Me: He's coming to live with us.

Nell: I beg your pardon.

Me: Dave is coming to live with us with...

Nell: With what? A fanfare?

Me: With his little sister Harriet.

Nell: His little sister Harriet?

Me: Yes.

Nell: This conversation will continue.

Me: I know.

Nell: The days of kindness are over. Things will be said.

Me: Yes.

Nell: Dave and Harriet.

Me: Yes.

Nell: I'm expecting a photo of Harriet.

Me: I will post one next time.

Nell: I knew that.

Me: Of course you did. Sorry.

CHAPTER 2:

Harriet

Nell: So this must be Harriet.

Me: Yes. Your little niece. Isn't she gorgeous?

Nell: Very tiny.

Me: Yes. She is a lot smaller than the others.

Nell: Others?

Me: There are eight of them, Nell, but don't worry—we know we can't have them all.

Nell: Good grief.

Me: Although I adored Freddy and Kev loved Fluffy.

Nell: Stop right now.

Me: You would love them too if you saw them.

Nell: But I didn't.

Me: No.

Nell: You went to my family home without me.

Me: We did.

Nell: You tore the family apart.

Me: That's a bit much, Nell. The puppies all have to go to new homes.

Nell: You do realise the implications of this. The weight of responsibility.

Me: Yes, of course. Kev and I know we will have a lot to do.

Nell: You? I'm talking about me. As their aunt I am going to be responsible for their upbringing.

Me: I suppose you are.

Nell: I didn't even have a say.

Me: No.

Nell: You never think things through.

Me: No.

Nell: Big Dave and Baby Harriet.

Me: Yes. But I know you will be wonderful with them.

Nell: Sometimes I think you forget I'm a Labrador, not Mary Poppins.

Me: Sorry.

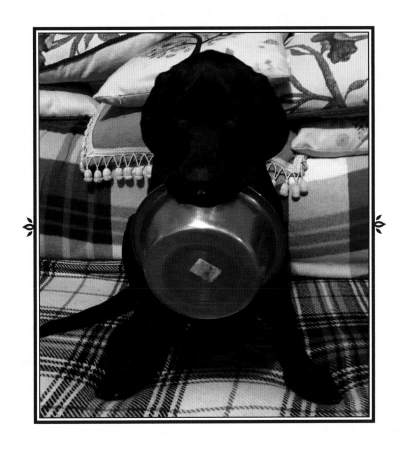

CHAPTER 3:

Adorable

Me: Nell, you have to come and look at Dave.

Nell: Why?

Me: He is absolutely adorable.

Nell: That isn't his bowl.

Me: I know.

Nell: His bowl is small.

Me: Yes, I know.

Nell: Because he is still a puppy.

Me: A giant puppy, but yes, you are right. But look, Nell; he is just like Oliver Twist saying, "Please, sir, can I have some more?"

Nell: I beg your pardon.

Me: You know. One of Dickens's most famous books. Dear little Oliver.

Nell: I know Dickens. Most Labradors do. I myself am named after one of his heroines, Little Nell. But David is not a poor, starving orphan, and he is certainly not little.

Me: How could anyone resist that little face.

Nell: David stole that bowl. It is mine.

Me: Perfect. Oliver was forced to steal by Fagin and the Artful Dodger.

Nell: I despair of you sometimes; I really do.

Me: Sorry.

Nell Sets the Scene

Nell: So David and Harriet joined the family and we all moved down south to live in Devon.

Me: Yes, we did.

Nell: Five dogs with you and Kev in a cottage near the sea.

Me: Yes.

Nell: Enjoying Spring. Leading a quiet life.

Me: Not that quiet.

Nell: Exactly. Just pass me a scone, please, and let's continue.

Me: Yes. Sorry.

PART 2:

Spring

CHAPTER 1:

Poppy's Scone
Recipe

Nell: Poppy has agreed to share her recipe for scones. Put your hat and apron on and come into the kitchen.

Me: I don't know where my hat is.

Nell: It's hanging on the hook next to everyone else's. You know Poppy insists on hats.

Me: Yes, I've got it.

Nell: The list of ingredients are:

- 225g/8oz/1 cup self raising flour, or plain flour with 1 level teaspoon/5ml baking powder

- 1/2 level teaspoon/2.5ml salt

- 50g/2oz margarine, or butter

- 25g/1oz caster sugar

- 125ml/4fl.oz/half a cup milk

- 1 egg

Me: I'll never remember that.

Nell: Just read our conversation later.

Me: Ok.

Nell: Now, Poppy is placing the flour and salt in a mixing bowl.

Me: Yes.

Nell: She has preheated the oven to 200C/400F.

Me: Thinking ahead.

Nell: Some of us do. Notice how she has cut the margarine, or butter if preferred, into small pieces and is rubbing them into the flour until it resembles breadcrumbs.

Me: Yes.

Nell: Poppy has poured the milk into a jug and is now mixing the egg into it and then adding to the flour, being careful to leave a little for later.

Me: Why is she stirring it with a fork?

Nell: It makes it lighter. The dough will be a soft consistency, not like pastry.

Me: It's quite gloopy isn't it?

Nell: Gloopy is not a word. I've told you this before.

Me: But we all use it and you know what I mean.

Nell: Poppy is now patting the dough down on to a floured board kneading it a little and then cutting out small rings, about the size of the top of an egg cup.

Me: I prefer a smaller scone too. It means I can have two.

Nell: The scones can be larger if you wish. Finally place on a lightly greased baking tray and brush with a little of the egg and milk mixture. Place in the oven at 200C/400F and bake for 15 mins.

Me: I can't wait.

Nell: When cool serve buttered, or not, with jam, preferably strawberry, and cream, preferably clotted.

Me: The Devon way is cream first and then jam. Even though I grew up in Devon I prefer the Cornish way which is jam first and then cream.

Nell: People must be allowed to decide for themselves.

Me: Yes, some may prefer no cream at all.

Nell: Now you are being ridiculous.

Me: Yes. Sorry.

POPPY'S SCONE RECIPE

INGREDIENTS:

- 225 g / 8 oz. / 1 cup self-raising flour, or plain flour with 1 level tsp. / 5 ml baking powder
- 1/2 level tsp. / 2.5 ml salt
- 50 g / 2 oz. margarine, or butter
- 25 g / 1 oz. caster sugar
- 125 ml / 4 fl. oz. / a half cup milk
- 1 egg

DIRECTIONS:

Place flour and salt in bowl.

Add margarine cut into small pieces.

Rub in with your fingertips until it is all like bread crumbs.

Mix egg with milk and add to flour, leaving a little bit over.

Stir with a fork. It will be a soft consistency, not like pastry.

Pat it down and put on a board.

Cut out small rings.

Brush with a little of the egg and milk so it goes a bit brown.

Put in oven at 190°C for 15 minutes.

Leave to cool a little.

Serve buttered (or not) with strawberry jam and clotted cream

Enjoy!

CHAPTER 2:

Waiting for Tony

Me: Where is Dave?

Nell: Quiet. David is working.

Me: On what?

Nell: On his Waiting Skills.

Me: How is he doing that?

Nell: It has come to my attention that David can be a little impatient.

Me: True.

Nell: So, he is outside waiting for Tony. Under my supervision, of course.

Me: Do you mean Tony, our postman?

Nell: Of course, I do. You know how David goes wild whenever Tony arrives.

Me: He does love Tony, and Tony loves him, to be fair. They are best mates.

Nell: That's as maybe, but David needs to try to learn to wait. A large part of a dog's life is spent waiting, and we, Labradors, pride ourselves on our patience.

Me: I'm not sure that's true, Nell.

I've seen you get very impatient.

Nell: Everyone has a bad day. Stop dwelling on the negatives.

Me: He's peering over the gate though, Nell, in quite an excited way.

Nell: Yes, I am aware. His task today is to try not to jump when Tony arrives. He may bark to alert us, but he has to try to remain calm.

Me: I'm not optimistic about this.

Nell: David may surprise us all.

Me: He's definitely going to surprise Tony when he sees that great big face looking over the gate.

Nell: Have faith. This is an important step in David's development.

Me: But what if he fails?

Nell: Then we will try again. A Labrador wasn't built in a day, you know.

Me: Don't you mean Rome?

Nell: I certainly do not. Now let's all wait for Tony.

Me: OK. Sorry.

CHAPTER 3:

Tony Is Back

Me: Look at those two. They are so pleased to see each other again.

Nell: Yes.

Me: Dave was counting the days until Tony got back from his holiday.

Nell: Yes, David marked it on his calendar and crossed each day off. Part of his Organisational Skills.

Me: I'm impressed.

Nell: They have a lot in common. Tony sings, you know.

Me: I did know. Sea shanties.

Nell: David loves singing.

Me: I'm not sure Dave's voice is quite up to it yet, Nell.

Nell: David is a quick learner. Maybe Tony can teach him.

Me: I used to sing in the school choir and Torquay Operatic Society.

Nell: That was a long time ago.

Me: What if you form your own group? I could be your manager.

Nell: I don't believe this.

Me: You can sing, Nell. I've heard you.

Nell: I have a pleasant contralto voice, that's true. Harriet is more of a soprano.

Me: Harriet sometimes sounds like a seagull.

Nell: Now, that is unkind, and you know perfectly well it's her "Are We Nearly at the Beach Yet?" voice. She can sing beautifully.

Me: Yes, I know.

Nell: Mutley is far too busy with his swing band, so don't bother him.

Me: What about Poppy?

Nell: I suppose we might persuade her to play her saxophone.

Me: There you are, then.

Nell: No, we aren't. Let's just organise singing lessons for David.

Me: OK.

Nell: Honestly, you will be entering us for *Britain's Got Talent* next.

Me: Now that's an idea.

Nell: Enough.

Me: Yes. Sorry.

CHAPTER 4:

St. George's Day

Me: Why is Dave shut in the back garden?

Nell: It's St. George's Day.

Me: What's that got to do with it?

Nell: We are reenacting the slaying of the dragon as part of the puppies' history lesson, and Dave is waiting for his entrance.

Me: Is Dave playing St. George, then?

Nell: Don't be silly. David is the dragon. We can't give him the sword.

Me: There's a sword?

Nell: Of course.

Me: I'm not sure that's a good idea, Nell. Someone could get hurt.

Nell: It's all perfectly safe. Poppy has been fencing for years.

Me: What? Is Poppy playing St. George?

Nell: Yes, she insisted. Mutley is the King, of course, and Harriet is his daughter, the Princess. That silly circlet of flowers you made me has actually come in useful. Harriet loves it.

Me: There's a big difference in size between Poppy and Dave.

Nell: Of course there is. Don't you know the story? It wouldn't be very believable if a huge St. George slayed a tiny little dragon, now would it?

Me: I suppose not. Dave won't be breathing fire, will he?

Nell: Don't be silly. He is a Labrador.

Me: Yes. Well, Happy St. George's Day, Nell.

Nell: Happy St. George's Day. Now, can we get on with rehearsals, please? The performance is at 3 p.m., and I haven't finished David's costume.

Me: Yes. Sorry.

St. George's Day

Saint George is the patron saint of England and St. George's Day is usually celebrated on 23rd April.

The legend of Saint George and the Dragon describes the real-life Saint George taming and slaying a dragon that demanded human sacrifices. Saint George rescues the princess who was chosen as the next offering.

CHAPTER 5:

Upsidedownmaddogface

Nell: You're tired today, aren't you?

Me: Yes, I am, Nell.

Nell: Got the cares of the world on your shoulders?

Me: I have a bit.

Nell: I know what will help.

Me: Do you?

Nell: My upside-down mad-dog face.

Me: Yes, that always makes me smile. I love you.

Nell: We love each other.

Me: Best friends.

Nell: We are.

Me: I could cuddle you all day.

Nell: No. There you go again invading my personal space.

Me: Oh dear.

Nell: How many times have I told you? Quit while you're ahead.

Me: I know.

Nell: Want to see my upside-down mad-dog face again?

Me: Yes, please.

Nell: Feeling better?

Me: Yes. Much.

Nell: See. It works every time. You only need to ask.

Me: Yes. Sorry.

CHAPTER 6:

I'm Having Second Thoughts about The Cat

Me: How was your tea?

Nell: I'm having second thoughts about The Cat.

Me: Oh dear.

Nell: It drank out of the milk jug and took all the smoked salmon.

Me: How rude?

Nell: Poppy had made sandwiches, and it took the salmon out and left us with the bread.

Me: Shocking.

Nell: Halfway through our game of bridge, it lit up a cigarette. In the house.

Me: That's not on.

Nell: I told it to go outside, of course, and it left. Just like that.

Me: Cats don't really care about convention.

Nell: Well, that's it, as I said to my friend Dorothy: "I'm not having that cat in my reading group."

Me: Do I know Dorothy?

Nell: She's a Salcombe setter. One of the sailing crowd.

Me: I didn't know you sailed.

Nell: Of course I sail. I learnt in Bembridge on the Isle of Wight. I used to do Cowes Week, but all that partying can be tiring.

Me: Yes.

Nell: Anyway, I can't stand here chatting all day. Herr Schäferhund, the German shepherd, is arriving at any moment to teach the puppies, and he needs his coffee. Hot and strong.

Me: Is he, now?

Nell: I beg your pardon?

Me: You like him. Admit it. You are wearing a new scarf, and is that perfume I can smell?

Nell: This old thing, and it's just my usual Chanel. Stop meddling and go and get the coffee.

Me: Yes. Sorry.

Sara Gets Excited

Me: It's about to get very exciting.

Nell: I know.

Me: It's hard to know who to trust.

Nell: I am aware. I was there, remember?

Me: Yes, of course. Sorry.

CHAPTER 7:
Who Is Siegfried Schäferhund?

Nell: I am afraid Siegfried Schäferhund might not be who he claims to be.

Me: Oh, Nell.

Nell: We had a lovely lunch by the sea. Lobster and champagne. But all he wanted to talk about was the Royal Wedding.

Me: That's odd.

Nell: He is supposed to be German, but sometimes he hardly has an accent at all.

Me: Yes, I had noticed.

Nell: I need to talk to him right now. Perhaps he can explain. Can you ask James to bring the car, please? I'm going to see him at the Thurlestone Hotel.

Me: Let me go with you.

Nell: No. I am doing this alone. Where is my handbag?

Me: Please be careful.

Nell: We shall see. I need to give him the chance to explain. The connection between us was real. I am sure it was.

Me: Take care, and call if you need me.

Nell: I will.

Me: I am so sorry.

CHAPTER 8:

Exposed

Nell: Well, at least I know it all now.

Me: Tell me everything. I have been so worried.

Nell: I arrived at the Thurlestone Hotel, and Siegfried was waiting for me. I had called from the car to let him know I was coming. When I saw his face, I could see the guilt in his eyes.

Me: Oh no.

Nell: I told him it was best to be honest with me, and he agreed.

Me: You were brave.

Nell: It turns out that Siegfried Schäferhund isn't his real name.

Me: Oh dear.

Nell: He isn't even German. It was all a lie. All part of the deception. I'm not quite sure I believe him even now.

Me: The bounder.

Nell: He is supposedly working undercover as a reporter for the *Daily Growl*. The farm dogs led him to me. He was trying to get a story on the royal family.

Me: What is his real name?

Nell: Charlie Shepherd, and he is from London. He started out as an actor but moved into journalism since it paid more. With his charm and acting skills, he managed to get a number of inside stories and became one of the *Daily Growl*'s lead reporters. I was his next target.

Me: What a cad, and as for those farm dogs!

Nell: Yes, indeed. No scones for them.

Me: It must have been such a shock.

Nell: To be honest, it was an even bigger shock when Poppy appeared in reception waving her sword, followed by David in his hat and Mutley in his dinner jacket.

Me: Gosh! How did they get there?

Nell: Harriet organised a taxi as soon as she heard I was going alone. She knew where he was staying, and put two and two together. Clever little thing. David and Poppy insisted she stayed behind, since she is still unwell. They were about to leave when Mutley arrived dressed to kill and got into the car. There is no arguing with him when he is determined, even if he could hear.

Me: I wish I had been there. What did Charlie do when they arrived?

Nell: He apologised and told them the same story. He said he had never meant to hurt anyone, especially the lovely Nelly, who had stolen his heart. His words.

Me: He called you Nelly?

Nell: Yes. Outrageous. It's Miss Eleanor Martin to him.

Me: Quite. What happened then?

Nell: Mutley told him to get on his bike. He can be quite forceful when riled.

Me: And did he?

Nell: Actually, he did. The Mercedes was rented, so he rode off on his motorbike, blowing me a farewell kiss.

Me: Gosh. The cheek of it.

Nell: Well, after that, I suggested they all join me in the bar for a stiff G and T to settle the nerves before James drove us home. David was a little squiffy when we got back, so I sent him upstairs for a lie down.

Me: Has Charlie gone back to London?

Nell: I don't know. I'm refusing to read his texts.

Me: You can't stay in contact with him, Nell. He's a scoundrel.

Nell: I shall do as I please, and what I please right now is to be left alone. I have a lot to think about.

Me: Yes. Sorry.

CHAPTER 9:

Stay Focused

Me: What a beautiful place.

Nell: Yes. Kev took me there yesterday for some quiet time. I've been feeling a little stressed.

Me: I know.

Nell: We had a gentle swim and a rest on the beach.

Me: Exactly what you needed.

Nell: We both enjoyed a delicious cool drink by the sea and discussed life and love. I was able to talk freely.

Me: You can do that with me, you know.

Nell: I know, but sometimes you just need to get away from it all. To gain some perspective.

Me: I agree, but it's always good to come back. When I smell the salt in the air, I know I am home.

Nell: You can't smell salt. I don't know how many times I've told you.

Me: I can.

Nell: It's the seaweed.

Me: I don't like seaweed.

Nell: That's not the point. Now, this might just be me, but have you noticed a Doberman recently?

Me: Where?

Nell: Just around. I've had a funny feeling in the last few days that I'm being followed.

Me: Followed?

Nell: Yes. And yesterday when we were at the beach, I thought I saw a Doberman in a dinghy.

Me: It might be on holiday.

Nell: Yes. But it was on its own. In my experience, they tend to travel in twos. It's probably just nerves after everything that's happened.

Me: Or an overactive imagination.

Nell: Something you would know all about. If you see it, let me know and don't approach it. I know what you are like.

Me: Have you told the others?

Nell: Yes. They are aware. Poppy had an unfortunate incident with a Doberman once, so she is on high alert.

Me: Good. I think. And Harriet?

Nell: Harriet is a huge comfort with her quiet ways. She is keeping her notebook with her so she can write down any sightings. I didn't ask Mutley, since the Doberman would have to walk up and tap him on the shoulder before he noticed.

Me: What about Dave?

Nell: David has gone to extremes again. The ridiculous animal has started wearing dark glasses and a trench coat with a pair of binoculars around his neck.

Me: Bless him.

Nell: This is not a game. I have a bad feeling, so please try to stay focused and don't let those farm dogs have any scones. Poppy has been baking, and they are hovering near the fence.

Me: Yes. Sorry.

CHAPTER 10:

Tony Is On Board

Nell: I feel better now that Tony is on board.

Me: Yes. He can keep a lookout when he is doing his rounds.

Nell: It was good to see him.

Me: He is a kind man.

Nell: Yes. Tony is to be trusted.

Me: I like sunny Sundays.

Nell: Yes. I've asked Poppy for boiled eggs for breakfast. David overindulged at the barbecue yesterday, so a light breakfast is called for.

Me: He was helping me with the clearing up.

Nell: He was stealing sausages.

Me: Poppy's sword dance worried me.

Nell: It worried everyone, especially when Mutley joined in. Did you notice that young farm dog trying to get Harriet's attention over the fence?

Me: No.

Nell: When I asked her about him, she giggled.

Me: She is adorable.

Nell: She is too young, and I am not having her seeing a farm dog. By the way, I'm sure the Doberman was behind me in the queue at the delicatessen yesterday morning. I had popped in to get Mutley's Cornish Yarg. He loves that cheese.

Me: Are you sure?

Nell: Yes. It's his favourite.

Me: I mean, are you sure it was the Doberman?

Nell: Yes. It was in the cooked-food section, but when I looked around it had gone.

Me: I wonder what it was buying.

Nell: What's that got to do with it?

Me: It might have revealed something about its situation. A large pork pie would imply there were more of them. A small one, that it is working alone.

Nell: I worry about you sometimes.

Me: I wonder what it wants, though. Do you think it's from the *Daily Growl*?

Nell: Charlie says it isn't. He says he has put a stop to it and told them to leave me alone. He was ridiculously concerned when I told him about the Doberman.

Me: I wish you wouldn't contact him.

Nell: It was just a quick message on Woof's App. Stop fussing. Soldiers, or triangles with your egg?

Me: Soldiers, please. But Nell . . .

Nell: Enough. I will be fine.

Me: Yes. Sorry.

CHAPTER 11:

Flooring

Me: Don't look at me like that.

Nell: What are they doing to the floor?

Me: They are laying the carpet upstairs and faux wood downstairs.

Nell: Carpet is soft under paw.

Me: Yes, that's why it is upstairs.

Nell: I wanted it downstairs too.

Me: It's not practical with all the sand and mud you lot bring in. We discussed this.

Nell: I wipe my paws.

Me: Well, that's what is happening, so please get off the chair so they can start.

Nell: It's obviously going to be one of those days.

Me: Why?

Nell: Poppy saw a Doberman when she was out jogging with Harriet early this morning.

Me: Oh no.

Nell: It smiled at them.

Me: That's nice.

Nell: No, it isn't. Dobermans don't smile. And it was eating a pork pie.

Me: Small or big?

Nell: It doesn't matter. It's the Doberman from the deli. I'm sure of it. Who eats a pork pie at 6 a.m.?

Me: I wish they would take Dave when they go jogging. It would be safer with Dobermans around.

Nell: David doesn't do early mornings, and he can't jog. He just runs really fast until he falls over like a llama. They have to climb over him, and it ruins their split times.

Me: Oh dear.

Nell: Actually, you are right. There may be more than one Doberman.

Me: You said they are usually in twos.

Nell: Exactly. I need Harriet to contact Richard Price and invite him for tea. He will know what to do.

Me: He's the sensible dog from the next village, isn't he? The poodle?

Nell: Richard Price is not a poodle. He is a pedigree black Russian terrier.

Me: Funny name for a Russian.

Nell: Richard is from Devon. His family runs the pub down by our beach. Labradors were originally from Newfoundland, but we aren't all Canadians.

Me: I like Canadians.

Nell: So do I, but that is not the point. Did David just go past me on a skateboard?

Me: Yes. Apparently it helps his balance, according to his surfing friends. Don't worry; Poppy has taken Mutley's board away.

Nell: Could you get my handbag, please. I feel a migraine coming on.

Me: Yes. Sorry.

CHAPTER 12:

The New Café

Me: You weren't very nice to Emily, and she gave you a treat.

Nell: Having your ears examined and that awful kennel cough vaccine is not my idea of fun.

Me: You didn't have to hide from her though. Did David know you were going to the vets, by the way?

Nell: Yes, I told him it was just routine, but he wouldn't believe me.

Me: I wondered why he was so upset.

Nell: I had lunch with the girls in town, and David was convinced I'd been poisoned by a Doberman.

Me: Why would he think that?

Nell: The farm dogs told him a Doberman was selling coffee on the Quay. Apparently it's taken over that old café and renamed it Starbarks. Silly name. It will never catch on.

Me: Was it selling pies?

Nell: Not as far as I know. I think it's mainly hot drinks with the odd muffin and sandwich. Food and drink for people on the go. You know the kind of thing.

Me: Sounds good. At least we know why the Doberman was here. It all makes sense now.

Nell: Does it?

Me: Yes. It tried a pie to see what the competition is like, and it smiled at Poppy because it was practising customer service.

Nell: And the sailing?

Me: Everyone needs time off.

Nell: You might actually be right. Maybe I just imagined it was following me.

Me: Shall we try a Starbarks coffee? I'm interested to see what it's like.

Nell: Certainly not. I'm not drinking out of a paper cup.

Me: But we could drink it by the sea and let the wind blow through our hair.

Nell: Is *Poldark* back on television by any chance?

Me: Yes.

Nell: I'm going to have to listen to you rambling on about Ross and Demelza for weeks now, aren't I?

Me: Yes.

Nell: Good grief.

Me: Sorry.

CHAPTER 13:

Keep It Safe

Nell: Well, this is all extremely confusing.

Me: Tell me what Dave said.

Nell: David got a phone call from Charlie during the party yesterday.

Me: How did he have his number?

Nell: They have been chatting quite a lot recently about motorbikes and football. David likes Charlie so much more now that he isn't Siegfried.

Me: I must say that Spain against Portugal football match was a bit of a corker.

Nell: A bit of a corker? Do speak English. Yes, it was rather exciting. Ronald took centre stage as usual.

Me: Ronaldo.

Nell: Anyway, do you want to know what Charlie said, or not?

Me: Yes.

Nell: Charlie told David to take my handbag and return it only after the party.

Me: Why?

Nell: I have no idea, but that's why I've only just got it back.

Me: How odd? I mean, Dave is always stealing your handbag. Maybe it was a joke. You need to give it a clean-out though, Nell. It's ever so full.

Nell: I do. No time like the present, I suppose.

Me: Yes. Does everyone still think the farm dogs spiked the drink?

Nell: Yes. Wretched animals drank it too, of course. They have no sense. What on earth is this at the bottom of my bag?

Me: What? Show me.

Nell: I've never seen it before.

Me: It's a man's cuff link. It's like a little clock. The time is wrong though. It's two hours ahead.

Nell: That's not the point. Where does it come from?

Me: I have no idea.

Nell: Ah! It has to be his. I'm going to call him right now.

Me: Who? Richard Price?

Nell: No. Richard Price wouldn't wear flashy cuff links. He is far too sensible. Charlie, of course. Quiet, it's ringing. He is answering. I'll take it outside.

Me: Nell, don't walk away. What is he saying? Come back. I hate waiting.

Nell: So, I was right. It is Charlie's. He said he is very sorry it is in my handbag, but I am to keep it safe, since it is extremely precious to him, and then he was gone.

Me: Curiouser and curiouser.

Nell: All right, Alice, you are not in Wonderland now. Let's watch *Saturday Kitchen*. All this intrigue is exhausting. It's only a cuff link. Can you ask Mutley to take that ridiculous moustache off, please? He is not Hercule Poirot.

Me: We thought it was funny. Sorry.

CHAPTER 14:
Just Another Sunday

Me: It was nice of The Cat to call round this morning.

Nell: I suppose so. Although I was in the middle of breakfast, and I like to read the Sunday papers in peace.

Me: The Cat wasn't to know.

Nell: I don't know why it thinks I would care whether there are new cats in the area.

Me: It seemed agitated.

Nell: I know. Cats are funny creatures. It kept telling me to watch my back.

Me: I think it was angling for a cup of tea.

Nell: It was angling for my scrambled egg and smoked salmon.

Me: Where is everyone?

Nell: Dave and Harriet are out in the garden playing badminton with the farm dogs. Poppy is cooking a roast, and Mutley is asleep in the sun. He does like a snooze in the hammock.

Me: Sounds like the perfect Sunday to me.

Nell: Except for those Dobermans on the hill.

Me: They are probably just out for a walk.

Nell: I saw one of them at the farm shop yesterday buying clotted cream. It waved at me.

Me: It was just being friendly.

Nell: You know they wanted Poppy's family recipe for scones. The cheek of it. They asked her when she went to Starbarks for her regular Americano.

Me: I hope she refused.

Nell: Of course. Wait. What was that?

Me: I can hear barking. A lot of barking. Are Dave and Harriet arguing with the farm dogs again? Why is Poppy running?

Nell: Those are frightened barks, and I can hear hissing and screaming. The puppies are in trouble. They need me now.

Me: Wait! Nell, be careful. I'm coming! Oh no! Let me help you. What's happened? Why are you looking like that?

Nell: It's too late. They have taken her.

Me: What?

Nell: Call the police. There have been injuries. Harriet has been kidnapped.

Me: No. Not little Harriet.

Nell: Stop wailing and call them now. There is no time to waste.

Me: Yes. Sorry.

CHAPTER 15:

Waiting for News

Me: Tell me again what happened.

Nell: I've been through it so many times now. With the police. With Richard Price on the phone. He didn't have to come straight over, by the way.

Me: He was worried, Nell, and he brought you flowers.

Nell: What good are flowers when Harriet is still missing? I know he means well, but I can't see anyone at the moment. Did you explain?

Me: Yes. He understood. He said to contact him anytime if you need him.

Nell: I will.

Me: Let's go through it again in case we've missed a vital clue.

Nell: David and Harriet were playing badminton over the fence with the farm dogs when a huge gang of cats appeared and leapt on Harriet. David rushed at them, but there were too many. They were crawling all over him, biting and scratching.

Me: Poor Dave is in a bad way. He can't forgive himself for not stopping them.

Nell: He was overpowered. The farm dogs jumped over the fence and tried to help, but the cats' claws were sharp and there were so many of them. That young farm dog with the floppy hair was hurt in the process.

Me: His name is Jim. He called round this morning asking for news. He was very upset. How did they capture Harriet?

Nell: The cats had a rope and a sack. Some of them held her down while the others tied her up and pushed her into the sack.

Me: And Mutley?

Nell: Mutley has a black eye. He fell out of the hammock when he heard the noise and rushed straight in to the fight, with no thought for his own safety. He did some damage from what I hear.

Me: He's such a brave old boy.

Nell: By the time Poppy and I realised what was happening, Harriet had gone.

Me: Dave is distraught, Nell. He won't stop crying. I don't know how to comfort him.

Nell: It's the puppies' birthday tomorrow. They will be a year old. I was planning a party. It's too much thinking of Harriet out there alone. She will be so frightened.

Me: She is stronger than we think. We will have a huge party when she comes home.

Nell: Yes. We have to think positively.

Me: Did you notice the Doberman?

Nell: Yes. It appears to be guarding our gate. I never thought I would say this, but it's strangely comforting.

Me: I agree. We will find Harriet soon. There are so many people looking for her. Everyone is pulling together.

Nell: Yes. I just wish I knew why she has been taken.

Me: Have you heard anything from Charlie? Dave keeps asking for him.

Nell: Nothing since that phone call. It's strange because I thought I saw him in the field.

Me: Surely he would tell you if he was here.

Nell: Yes. I was probably mistaken. We will just have to wait and hope the kidnappers get in touch. Stop crying. You are not helping. Harriet is a Labrador, and Labradors don't give in.

Me: Yes. Sorry.

CHAPTER 16:

Tell Nobody

Me: Nell, what is it?

Nell: They've just sent me a photo of Harriet. It's heartbreaking. They must have my number. How did they get it? My poor little Harriet. She must be so afraid, and it is her birthday today.

Me: This is dreadful, but at least we know she is alive. Was there a message?

Nell: No. Just the photo. I better show the police, I suppose. I don't want David to see it. He hasn't stopped crying since Harriet was taken.

Me: Wait. Nell, your phone is ringing.

Nell: No caller ID. It might be them. "Yes. This is Nell. Where is she? What do you want? But I don't have anything. Yes, I will. Please don't hurt Harriet!"

Me: What did they say?

Nell: They said, "You have something of ours, and now we have something of yours. Await further instructions. Tell nobody."

Me: What do they mean? What do we have?

Nell: I don't know. What could they want from us? We don't have any money, but we can raise some if we have to. They said we have something of theirs. What can it be?

Me: Should we tell the police?

Nell: Too risky. We are going to have to do this alone.

Me: Nell, your phone is ringing again!

Nell: "Yes, it's Nell. Where are you? They've taken Harriet. You knew? All right. I'll see you then."

Me: Who was that?

Nell: It was Charlie. He knew about Harriet. He wants to see me. He's coming over now.

Me: Oh my goodness. What if he is dangerous?

Nell: We have to get Harriet back. Charlie knows something, and I am going to find out what it is.

Me: Be careful.

Nell: Ask Poppy and Mutley to join me. They need to know Charlie is on his way. David can stay watching the football, and you must keep an eye on him. Tell Poppy to bring her sword.

Me: I'm not sure that's wise.

Nell: We have gone beyond wise. Just look at that photo.

Me: Yes. Sorry.

This Is Such a Worry

Me: I think I need a lie down.

Nell: Just drink your Earl Grey.

Me: Our little Harriet. Kidnapped.

Nell: Can we read on now?

Me: Yes. Sorry.

CHAPTER 17:

Charlie Explains

Me: Has Charlie gone?

Nell: Yes, for now.

Me: Dave was so pleased to see him, and he seems to have calmed down.

Nell: Yes. Charlie promised him that his sister will be home soon. Now, you are going to have to sit down. I know what you are like, so take a deep breath and don't fuss, just listen.

Me: Does he know where Harriet is?

Nell: No, he doesn't, but he is sure she is nearby and we will find her soon.

Me: How can he know that?

Nell: Charlie is not a journalist. He works for the British Secret Service.

Me: Do you mean MI5? Is Charlie a spy?

Nell: Yes. Apparently it all started at the Royal Wedding. A Russian double agent was supposed to exchange classified material.

The exchange went wrong, and he ended up putting it in my handbag.

Me: A Russian double agent? Your handbag?

Nell: Yes. Strange little man. I remember him now. I dropped my handbag and he picked it up.

Me: It's the cuff link!

Nell: Yes. He managed to get a message to MI5, telling them what he had done and describing me and the handbag. They checked the security camera footage of the wedding and tracked me down.

Me: What happened then?

Nell: Charlie was sent in to get it.

Me: Why didn't he take it? He had plenty of opportunities when he was pretending to be Siegfried.

Nell: While he was here he received information that there was a mole in MI5, so he decided to leave the cuff link with me to see if the mole would try to get it.

Me: We are talking double agents now, aren't we? Informants, not animals?

Nell: Good grief! Of course we are.

Me: And that's why you still have the cuff link? I don't want it here. Get rid of it.

Nell: No. It has forced them to show their hand. The cuff link contains a list of double agents. It will lead Charlie to the mole.

Me: But what about Harriet? It's terrible that she is being used in all this.

Nell: I know. Charlie apologised. He and the Dobermans were monitoring us, but they hadn't counted on the cats moving so quickly.

Me: So the Dobermans are part of MI5?

Nell: Yes. Charlie wasn't sure at first if one of the Dobermans was the

mole, which is why he warned me to keep away from them.

Me: And The Cat?

Nell: The Cat is innocent. It tried to warn us.

Me: Does he have an idea who the mole is?

Nell: I think he does. He has asked me to trust him and wait for them to get in touch. He has promised me that we will get Harriet back very soon. I don't know why, but I believe him.

Me: So all we can do is wait?

Nell: Yes. He needs to unmask the mole, and Harriet is the key.

Me: So Charlie is like James Bond? Ruthless but charming. Breaking hearts and risking innocent lives.

Nell: James Bond is a fictional character, Miss Moneypenny. We are close to rescuing Harriet. Focus on that.

Me: Yes. Sorry.

CHAPTER 18:
Come Alone

Nell: Charlie says I am to expect a phone call. Things are starting to move, and he thinks they will be in touch.

Me: I am dreadfully worried about this, Nell. Are you sure we shouldn't tell the police?

Nell: No police.

Me: Oh my goodness, Nell. Your phone is ringing.

Nell: Give it to me. "Yes. Nell speaking. I want to talk to Harriet first. No, I need to talk to her."

Me: Is it them?

Nell: Yes. They are getting her.

Me: I can't bear this.

Nell: Quiet! "Harriet, it's me, Auntie Nell. Are you OK? We are going to get you out of there. We promise. We love you too. Yes. Of course you can. Anything you want. I will. He's fine; it was just a black eye. Who? Yes. Be brave. Not long now. Harriet!"

Me: What happened?

Nell: She's gone.

Me: What did she say? Is she OK?

Nell: Hush! It's them again. "Yes. I'm still here. Where? What time? Completely alone? Yes. OK. I will be there."

Me: Tell me.

Nell: Harriet sounded tired but determined. She says she is OK and asked if she can still have a birthday cake when she comes home. Bless her. She sends her love to us all. She says to tell David she is thinking of him all the time, and they will celebrate their birthday together. She was worried about Mutley and sent special love to Jim. Who on earth is Jim?

Me: The floppy-haired farm dog. He tried to save her. Remember?

Nell: Oh yes.

Me: What did they say?

Nell: They told me to meet them on Bantham Beach at 5 a.m. tomorrow. I have to bring the cuff link, and I must be alone. They will bring Harriet. I am to walk toward them along the beach.

Me: You can't go alone, Nell.

Nell: I can and I will. James can drop me at the car park and wait for me there.

Me: But Nell . . .

Nell: I am bringing Harriet home tomorrow, and I am going alone. No arguments. It's something I have to do.

Me: OK. Sorry.

CHAPTER 19:

Harriet Is Free

Me: You did it! She is free!

Nell: When she came running along the beach toward me, my heart stopped. It was wonderful. My darling Harriet. Where is she now?

Me: She's with Dave and the others in the kitchen. She is quite safe. She has a soft blanket and Dave to cuddle. You sit down, and I'll get you some tea. You look exhausted.

Nell: I am, but a cup of Earl Grey and one of Poppy's scones will soon sort me out.

Me: Poppy says she will bring a tray in. She is just making Harriet some warm milk. Dave drank the first bowl by mistake.

Nell: It's been a long week. Is Charlie still here?

Me: He and the head Doberman have a few things to sort out. He said he will be in touch.

Nell: Yes. John is a charming Doberman. Very polite and softly spoken.

Me: Are you able to tell me what happened?

Nell: I hardly know how to put it into words. The shock. The awful shock when he came toward me with Harriet.

Me: Start at the beginning.

Nell: James dropped me off, and I walked down to the beach. I could make out some figures at the other end, and so I started walking toward them. The sea mist was quite thick, so I couldn't see them properly. I was holding the cuff link as agreed.

Me: You must have been terrified.

Nell: I was. As I drew nearer, I saw Harriet. She had a rope around her neck, and he was holding it in his teeth.

Me: Who?

Nell: Richard Price! It was Richard Price!

Me: No!

Nell: He was surrounded by hissing cats. I could hardly breathe, but I kept on walking.

Me: So brave.

Nell: Suddenly there was the sound of barking, and Charlie leapt out of the sea followed by a whole army of Dobermans. They had been hiding behind the rocks.

Me: Good for Charlie!

Nell: The cats fled when they saw the Dobermans, and Richard Price dropped the rope. That's when Harriet broke free and ran toward me.

Me: Oh my goodness. Did he chase her?

Nell: No. He didn't get the chance. Charlie pinned him to the ground, and the Dobermans formed a circle around them. Richard Price wasn't going anywhere.

Me: The villain!

Nell: Yes. Charlie tied him up, and he and the Dobermans took him away. Harriet and I just clung to each other.

Me: I bet you did.

Nell: We were watching them go when there was a triumphant bark behind us, and David came rushing over the sand dunes wearing his hat.

Me: Bless him.

Nell: Closely followed by Poppy with her sword.

Me: Of course.

Nell: And Mutley in his DJ carrying a picnic basket. It was a wonderful sight. Harriet burst into tears, and so did I. David knocked her over with kisses as usual, but she didn't care.

Me: What a relief.

Nell: Fortunately, Poppy had a flask of sweet tea in the basket and the birthday cake she made yesterday. Harriet wolfed it all down with David's help. The poor little thing was starving.

Me: I bet she was.

Nell: I could only manage some tea. Mutley fortified mine with a little brandy and drank his straight from the bottle.

Me: I'm not surprised.

Nell: We all just sat on the beach together looking at the sun rising over the sea and holding Harriet close. A special moment.

Me: I can imagine.

Nell: But what were they all doing there? I told them not to come.

Me: We were never going to let you go alone, Nell. Charlie told us what to do.

Nell: You just don't listen, do you?

Me: Not this time, and no, I'm not sorry.

PART 3:

Summer

CHAPTER 1:
Nell's Strawberry and Raspberry Pavlova Recipe

Nell: Poppy is making my favourite summer dessert today. Strawberry and Raspberry Pavlova.

Me: My mother used to make it.

Nell: Yes. She made the best meringues, and I always think of her when I eat this.

Me: So do I.

Nell: Pavlova is made with meringue, fruit, and cream, so we have divided the ingredients into two.

Me: OK.

Nell: For the meringue:

- 4 egg whites
- 250 g / 8 oz. caster sugar
- 1 tsp. white wine vinegar
- 1 tsp. corn flour

Me: I see.

Nell: For the topping:

- 500 g / 16 oz. fresh strawberries, hulled and halved
- 250 g / 8 oz. fresh raspberries
- 1 tbsp. icing sugar
- 350 ml / 10 oz. double cream

Me: So not fattening at all.

Nell: If you are going to eat a dessert, then do it properly.

Me: True.

Nell: So now for the method:

- Poppy has heated the oven to 150°C / 130°C fan or 300°F / 250°F fan.

- She has placed a dinner plate on some baking paper and is drawing a circle around the plate with a pencil.

- She is now whisking her 4 egg whites in the mixer until they form stiff peaks, and then adding 250 g / 8 oz. caster sugar 1 tbsp. at a time until the meringue is thick and glossy.

- Finally, she adds 1 tsp. white wine vinegar and 1 tsp. corn flour.

- You may spread the meringue inside the circle she has drawn, and make the sides a little higher than the middle, please, like a crater.

Me: Is that right?

Nell: Yes. Now we will bake it for 1 hour and then turn off the heat and let the Pavlova cool completely inside the oven.

Me: How long will that take, only I am starving?

Nell: I don't know. Let's go down to the beach for a swim until it is cool.

Me: It's been hours. Poppy says it is ready now.

Nell: Yes. She is whipping 350 ml / 10 oz. double cream with 1 tsp. icing sugar and spreading it over the meringue. She is then adding 500 g / 16 oz. strawberries and 250 g / 8 oz. raspberries on top. It is ready to be served.

Me: It looks wonderful. Let's get stuck in.

Nell: Certainly not. We will savour each mouthful. Pavlova is best enjoyed in the garden on a summer's day, possibly with a glass of chilled champagne, not gobbled up in the kitchen.

Me: Yes, of course. Sorry.

NELL'S STRAWBERRY AND RASPBERRY PAVLOVA RECIPE

INGREDIENTS:

- 4 egg whites
- 250 g / 8.8 oz. / 1.1 cups caster sugar
- 1 tsp. / 5ml white wine vinegar
- 1 tsp. / 5ml corn flour
- 500 g / 17.6 oz. / 2.2 cups fresh strawberries, hulled and halved
- 250 g / 9oz. fresh raspberries
- 1 tsp. /5 ml icing sugar
- 350 ml / 12 oz. double cream

METHOD

Heat oven to 150°C / 130°C fan / gas 2.
Using a pencil, mark out the circumference of a dinner plate on baking parchment.

Whisk egg whites with a hand mixer until they form stiff peaks, then whisk in caster sugar, 1 tbsp. at a time, until the meringue looks glossy.

Whisk in white wine vinegar and corn flour.

Spread the meringue inside the circle, creating a crater by making the sides a little higher than the middle.

Bake for 1 hour, then turn off the heat and let the Pavlova cool completely inside the oven.

When the meringue is cool, whip double cream with 1 tsp. icing sugar and spread it over the meringue.

Put hulled and halved strawberries and raspberries on the cream.

Serve and enjoy.

CHAPTER 2:

Best Friend

Me: I wonder what made you so wise, Nell.

Nell: I prefer to call it common sense.

Me: Whatever it is, we need more of it, if you ask me. Except people don't. They usually ask you. Why is that, do you think?

Nell: I can't imagine.

Me: Someone applied to be your personal assistant.

Nell: I know.

Me: I would be ever so good at that, you know.

Nell: Would you?

Me: Yes. I could make tea and stuff.

Nell: You could.

Me: And other things too.

Nell: You don't know what a PA does, do you?

Me: Not really.

Nell: Harriet got the job.

Me: Oh.

Nell: She is bright and sensible.

Me: Yes.

Nell: She will be perfect.

Me: Yes, you are right.

Nell: You are my best friend, though.

Me: I am?

Nell: Of course you are. Where would I be without you? Now, we need Earl Grey and shortbread, since we've got a lot to discuss.

Me: Yes.

Nell: David has applied to be my press secretary.

Me: Well, he's ever so friendly and awfully keen.

Nell: It's a dreadful idea. Don't be so silly.

Me: Yes, sorry.

CHAPTER 3:

Tony Pays a Visit

Me: There is nothing like a surprise visit from your best friend.

Nell: I agree. It is a joy to see them together.

Me: The minute Dave saw Tony, he ran to the gate.

Nell: Yes. Although running isn't actually allowed after his injury. They had a marvellous discussion about bandages, and David showed Tony his. Tony's lab, Milo, had chickens on his bandage.

Me: And Dave's?

Nell: David's has tractors. In honour of grandson Jonathan, I expect, we know how much he loves them.

Me: Yes, although I'm not sure the vet knew that when he put it on.

Nell: I am aware of that, but Jonathan isn't.

Me: Yes.

Nell: Both Mutley and Jonathan have birthdays this month. Mutley on the 18th and Jonathan on the 19th.

Me: They do.

Nell: And I believe you also became a great aunt on Wednesday to little Lily.

Me: I did.

Nell: So all in all, this is quite a busy month.

Me: It is.

Nell: I know it would have been your mother's birthday this month too.

Me: Yes.

Nell: We will still celebrate her life.

Me: Yes, we will.

Nell: In the meantime, let's enjoy the fact that Tony's visit has made David's day.

Me: Yes. Sorry.

Nell: There is no need to say sorry. None at all.

CHAPTER 4:

Canvassing

Me: Who are those three waiting for?

Nell: Substitute Tony.

Me: Who?

Nell: Tony is on holiday, so there is a different postman this week.

Me: Dave will be missing him.

Nell: Yes, but as I told David, everyone needs a break, and Tony works very hard. Anyway, David has enough to occupy him at the moment.

Me: Why?

Nell: He and Harriet are working on the campaign.

Me: This isn't the beaches thing again, is it?

Nell: What do you mean, the beaches thing? As campaign manager I object to that, but it's not surprising, I suppose, since you are from the opposition.

Me: No, I'm not. I'm actually on your side, Nell. I don't think dogs should be banned from the beach from May until October.

Nell: Speak to my deputy then; there may be something you can do.

Me: Is Mutley your deputy?

Nell: Of course not. Poppy is my deputy. There is no point in speaking to Mutley. He can't hear.

Me: He can hear a little.

Nell: He is nearly 15. Give him a break. Anyway, Mutley is executive chairman, so any applications to him must be made in writing.

Me: I see.

Nell: Just talk to Poppy; there are bound to be some envelopes that need addressing. Now let me finish my speech. Radio Devon are due here soon.

Me: OK. Sorry.

Local Radio

Me: I love listening to our local BBC Radio Devon

Nell: They interviewed you, didn't they?

Me: Yes, about naughty dogs.

Nell: I hope you told them you don't know any.

Me: I might have mentioned Dave. Sorry.

CHAPTER 5:

Partying until Dawn

Me: What is wrong with Dave? He seems ever so tired.

Nell: Don't get me started.

Me: Oh dear.

Nell: Partying with Poppy until dawn.

Me: Oh no.

Nell: Dancing in the garden.

Me: Gosh.

Nell: Drinking from the plant pots.

Me: Oh my.

Nell: And rapping with the farm dogs.

Me: What?

Nell: Oh yes. Goodness only knows what the repercussions will be.

Me: He is young, though, Nell, and it's a bank holiday.

Nell: What's Poppy's excuse, then? She is five.

Me: Poppy is a rebel.

Nell: Well, she's a rebel without a sword. Because I've hidden it.

Me: She won't like that.

Nell: And David is grounded until further notice. When he finally came to bed, he was wearing the farmer's cap. How am I going to explain that?

Me: Where is Harriet?

Nell: She and Mutley are checking the *Daily Growl*. We need to know what has been said.

Me: They were only partying, Nell. Surely that's not newsworthy.

Nell: No, silly, about my beach campaign. Do keep up.

Me: Yes, of course. Sorry.

CHAPTER 6:

Together Again

Nell: It's good to be home. Pass me the Sunday papers, would you? I must say Poppy has excelled herself with these croissants. Delicious.

Me: Yes. The jam is yummy. Is it Poppy's?

Nell: No. Farmers market. There's a very pleasant golden retriever who grows her own fruit.

Me: Well, it's lovely.

Nell: I am looking forward to a quiet day and Poppy's roast. I chose chicken. Organic, free range.

Me: Farmers market?

Nell: No, from the farm next door.

Me: Jim will have made sure it's a good one. He always wants the best for Harriet.

Nell: She is still very young, and he is a farm dog. They come from two different worlds.

Me: We had a lovely time on the beach yesterday evening, didn't we? Dave just ran and ran. He was so happy.

Nell: Yes. David was in his element. Exciting as it is to travel, there is nothing like coming home.

Me: Very true.

Nell: As I said to the puppies, "Home is not a place. It's a feeling." However far away we might travel, our hearts will always be here.

Me: You are right. My heart has always stayed in Devon, and when we moved here it felt like coming home.

Nell: Exactly. On another note, Mutley hasn't invited The Cat again, has he? Only last night's karaoke was too much. Whatever possessed The Cat and David to sing "Barcelona"?

Me: I quite liked it.

Nell: But all those sequins, and David was wearing a moustache? Whatever next?

Me: Don't worry. The Cat is visiting an aunt in Truro.

Nell: Just us then. Perfect.

Me: Actually, there is someone else. He called while you were away, and I suggested he visit today.

Nell: Who?

Me: Charlie.

Nell: Where's my handbag? I need to look my best. Stop smiling like a dog who's got the biscuit. Tell Poppy we have an extra guest for lunch, and ask Harriet to come and brush my hair. You had to interfere, didn't you?

Me: Yes. Sorry.

CHAPTER 7:

Mutley's 15th Birthday

Nell: Would someone please get Gladys the Black Pomeranian out of the hamper. She has her head in the Stilton.

Me: You wouldn't let her sleep in your handbag.

Nell: Rita Pawreno the dancing Chihuahua is already in there. Why has Ron Gilbert, the Great Dane from Torquay, got a moustache?

Me: The Cat painted it on him while he was asleep.

Nell: Well, Mutley's 15th-birthday party is one we shall never forget.

Me: The highlight has to be Mutley singing "My Way" on top of the piano.

Nell: Yes. It's amazing what a swing band and a bowl of jam roly-poly can do.

Me: What about Poppy doing a sword dance?

Nell: Accompanied by John the Doberman on the bagpipes. Their kilts were the genuine article, you know.

Me: When those Frenchies started flamenco dancing, I couldn't believe my eyes.

Nell: Yes. I never knew bulldogs could be so light on their paws.

Me: Harriet and Jim sang beautifully. She has such a sweet voice.

Nell: I'm not sure we needed Rita and Gladys dancing around them with roses in their teeth.

Me: And Dave's performance? Spectacular.

Nell: Words fail me. Where did he get those stilts from, and the trapeze?

Me: And how did The Cat get in the cake?

Nell: I've no idea, but when it jumped out at midnight I thought that elderly Airedale in the corner was going to have a heart attack.

Me: It was very impressive. Mutley loved it all.

Nell: And we love Mutley.

Me: Talking of love. Did I see you smoochy dancing with Charlie?

Nell: Smoochy dancing? Go and wish Mutley a happy birthday again from us all, and leave my love life to me.

Me: Yes. Sorry.

Stop Interfering

Me: You and Charlie.

Nell: What are you talking about?

Me: Love at first sight.

Nell: Just concentrate on reading and leave my love life to me.

Me: Yes. Sorry.

CHAPTER 8:

The Secret Beach

Me: I don't like Mondays. They get me down.

Nell: Just think of the secret beach.

Me: Yes. It's a special place.

Nell: It is. Sometimes when the world is getting you down, you just need to go there in your mind.

Me: Very true.

Nell: I like the fact that hardly anyone knows it is there.

Me: So do I.

Nell: Getting there isn't easy.

Me: No, it isn't.

Nell: But once you are there, it is all worthwhile.

Me: Are we really talking about the secret beach, or is this some kind of metaphor?

Nell: Metaphor? It's Monday; give me a break.

Me: I just wondered.

Nell: Have a cup of tea, look at the photos, and think of happy times.

Me: OK, sorry.

CHAPTER 9:

Petunia

Nell: What is your grandson Jonathan doing?

Me: He and Seamus were searching for Petunia. She needed to go to bed.

Nell: Was she a guest of your sister Charlotte's too?

Me: No, she lives there.

Nell: When are you bringing Jonathan and Alice home?

Me: We should be back by the afternoon. Any news?

Nell: Mutley managed to ward off Barker King's attempted takeover of Pizza Mutt, but now he is having issues with his hypermarket.

Me: I didn't know he had one.

Nell: Walbarks. You might have heard of it. Anyway, apparently he told the shareholders he was sorry, but Jonathan was visiting and he needed to get home. He has his priorities right.

Me: Yes.

Nell: Oh, the big news is John proposed to Poppy.

Me: Gosh.

Nell: Yes, but she turned him down. Said she wasn't ready.

Me: Is he awfully disappointed?

Nell: He says he is prepared to wait. Did Jonathan find Petunia?

Me: Eventually. She was under the shed. She refused to come out. Alice poked her with a stick. We had to leave her there overnight.

Nell: I'm not sure that is the way to treat guests.

Me: Petunia is a chicken.

Nell: You could have mentioned that before. Just drive home now, please. We miss you.

Me: Yes. Sorry.

CHAPTER 10:

Who Ate My Slipper?

Me: Somebody ate the end of my slipper.

Nell: We are aware, and the culprit has confessed.

Me: It's the second pair. This time it's the toe, and last time it was the heel.

Nell: Yes. The culprit regrets what has happened and will endeavour not to do it again.

Me: It was taken while I was asleep.

Nell: There is no point in dwelling on it. We all need to move on.

Me: It wasn't you, was it?

Nell: What kind of question is that?

Me: Are you going to tell me who it was?

Nell: There is no need.

Me: You wouldn't be like this if I ate your slipper.

Nell: True. I would be extremely concerned about your state of mind.

Me: You know what I mean.

Nell: Let's all move on and put this incident behind us. It was a moment of madness.

Me: I know it was one of the puppies.

Nell: Actually you don't, and they are adolescents.

Me: Mutley would never eat my shoe, and neither would Poppy.

Nell: I agree.

Me: Sometimes I think you enjoy annoying me.

Nell: Don't be ridiculous. The matter has been dealt with internally.

Me: I hate not knowing.

Nell: Just rise above it. We have menus to go through with Poppy, and The Cat has created a mood board for the café.

Me: Just tell me.

Nell: We've decided to drop the raisin scones because of the dangers to dogs.

Me: But I need to know.

Nell: Labradors stick together. Pocket money will go toward new slippers. That's all you need to know.

Me: Yes. Sorry.

CHAPTER 11

Jonathan Sky Is Two Today

Jonathan Sky is two today.

Nell says: "Dance and shout 'Hurrah.'"

Nell says: "Go and chew a shoe

Because Jonathan Sky has just turned two."

Mutley and Poppy,

Harriet and Dave

Are bouncing around

And giving a wave.

Charlie and Jim,

Malcolm and John,

Gladys and Rita,

The Cat and big Ron.

Granny and Grandpa

Have stories to tell.

So just keep on reading

Conversations with Nell.

Listen very carefully

And know this is true.

We love you Jonathan Sky

Happy Birthday to you.

CHAPTER 12:

Prawns

Me: What have Poppy and Mutley been doing?

Nell: Chasing flamingos.

Me: Flamingos? In our garden.

Nell: Yes. But that's not the strange thing.

Me: It isn't?

Nell: My friend Valerie and I picked up some prawns from Sid the Fish yesterday.

Me: That's not strange.

Nell: No. Although some people find the fact that Sid is an otter rather odd. We needed them because Poppy was going to make prawn sandwiches for lunch today.

Me: Still, not strange.

Nell: She took the prawns out of the fridge this morning, ready to shell, and left them to put some bread in the oven. When she returned they had gone.

Me: The prawns?

Nell: No. The shells.

Me: Someone was being very helpful.

Nell: Yes. There was a small flamingo sitting in the kitchen, eating shells.

Me: Now, that is strange.

Nell: Well, even though Poppy was understandably perplexed, she remained polite.

Me: Good for her.

Nell: She asked the flamingo what it was doing in her kitchen eating prawn shells.

Me: I don't blame her. Did it answer?

Nell: Oh yes. It said its name was Malcolm, and it was desperate for prawns.

Me: Why didn't it just eat them all?

Nell: Apparently Malcolm is a very polite flamingo. He felt it only fair to leave Poppy the actual prawns.

Me: That is polite.

Nell: Poppy thought so too, so she made Malcolm some tea and gave him the rest of the prawns.

Me: Good.

Nell: Unfortunately the other flamingos tracked Malcolm down and started flying around, shouting. We think they used Find my iBone.

Me: Probably.

Nell: Well, Poppy wasn't having it, so she and Mutley chased them away.

Me: Where is Malcolm?

Nell: In the kitchen finishing the prawns.

Me: Of course he is. Silly me. Sorry.

Home Truths

Me: I love a good prawn.

Nell: It's never actually just one though,
is it?

Me: No, once I start it is difficult to stop.

Nell: Isn't that the truth?

Me: Yes. Sorry.

CHAPTER 13:

What Are We Going to Do about Malcolm?

Nell: I was just explaining to Harriet that Malcolm probably can't stay.

Me: Why? I don't think I have ever met a more polite flamingo in my life.

Nell: You don't know any other flamingos.

Me: I know the ones that keep shouting outside.

Nell: They want Malcolm to come home.

Me: I don't think Malcolm wants to go home.

Nell: Harriet agrees with you. She and Malcolm had a heart-to-heart last night.

Me: Did they?

Nell: Yes. Apparently Malcolm's heart is not in it. He is struggling with being a real flamingo. He is so much smaller and quieter.

Me: He loved it when Dave and The Cat danced the samba.

Nell: Yes. But a real flamingo would have joined in. Malcolm was much happier watching from the sidelines.

Me: Maybe that's why he wears glasses.

Nell: What on earth are you talking about? He wears glasses because he is shortsighted.

Me: Where is he now?

Nell: Helping Poppy prepare the Sunday roast. We are having chicken.

Me: He's not going to eat one of his own, Nell.

Nell: Of course he isn't. Poppy is making him a crab risotto. One of the Dartmouth dachshunds had a crab to spare, so David's driven over to pick it up on his motorbike.

Me: Did Gladys go in the sidecar?

Nell: Yes, and The Cat. It's the Dartmouth Food Fair, so they are having a look around while they are there.

Me: Good idea.

Nell: Harriet says life is tough for the lesser flamingos. The greater flamingos boss them around.

Me: I think he should be allowed to stay.

Nell: Mutley is going to have a quiet word with him after lunch. He will report back, and there will be a family vote.

Me: I'm voting for Malcolm.

Nell: Have you considered the fact that Malcolm might be a spy?

Me: Isn't he too pink and polite to be a spy?

Nell: I'm not even going to answer that question.

Me: Sorry.

CHAPTER 14:

Macarons

Me: Where is Poppy?

Nell: Having a lie in.

Me: Poppy never has a lie in, and it's Monday.

Nell: She and Malcolm were up until the early hours making macarons.

Me: I'm glad we decided that Malcolm can stay.

Nell: Yes. We still have to meet with the Count to secure Malcolm's release.

Me: Why? Was Malcolm a prisoner?

Nell: No. Malcolm foolishly signed up to the Flamingo foreign legion.

Me: He did?

Nell: Yes; I can't think what possessed him to do such a thing. They are renowned for their brutality.

Me: Gosh.

Nell: Malcolm's father and brothers served, so I presume it was expected of him.

Me: I'm surprised he got in.

Nell: True. Anyway, the Count has agreed to meet us this afternoon.

Me: Who is the Count?

Nell: Do you mean you have never heard of Count Bingo Flamingo?

Me: No, and it's a very silly name.

Nell: Bingo is greatly feared and a ruthless soldier.

Me: What if Bingo refuses?

Nell: He won't. Mutley and I will see to that, and Poppy has her sword with John the Doberman on standby.

Me: No wonder she is having a lie in.

Nell: Malcolm is extremely nervous, so no silly talk.

Me: Where is he?

Nell: Harriet is teaching him how to knit; she learnt it from the visiting Welsh corgis. She will be at Malcolm's side during negotiations.

Me: Will Dave be on his other side?

Nell: Certainly not. David will be singing, and Gladys will perform a contemporary dance.

Me: Of course. Sorry.

CHAPTER 15:

Bingo

Me: Nell, can I have a word?

Nell: I'm resting in the broken chair.

Me: I know, but I wanted to hear about yesterday's meeting.

Nell: Well, the first shock was Count Bingo's size.

Me: Was he dreadfully portly?

Nell: Good grief. Have you ever seen a portly flamingo? They are all feathers and spindly legs. No, he was extremely tall.

Me: Gosh. And Malcolm is so small.

Nell: Malcolm is a lesser flamingo. I confess I wasn't expecting Count Bingo to have a French accent, either, or that he would be wearing a monocle.

Me: I suppose that is a little unusual.

Nell: Anyway, Poppy presented her case, explaining that Malcolm's heart wasn't in fighting, but he had a passion for cooking and she was willing to take him on as a trainee sous chef.

Me: Where was Malcolm?

Nell: Hiding behind John the Doberman in a bulletproof, sequinned vest made by The Cat.

Me: What did Count Bingo say?

Nell: He was not best pleased until Harriet offered him a macaron and David started singing, "Non, je ne regrette rien."

Me: I didn't know he could sing in French.

Nell: Yes. David has a vast repertoire. When he moved on to "Joe, le taxi" and Gladys began her contemporary dance, the Count was completely mesmerised.

Me: I bet he was.

Nell: Gladys was wearing pink feathers, which was a clever idea.

Me: Yes.

Nell: And then something strange happened.

Me: Surely not.

Nell: Count Bingo joined in, whirling Gladys across the floor.

Me: Gosh.

Nell: And then he stopped. Put his monocle back in his eye, bowed, and left.

Me: So is Malcolm free?

Nell: A young flamingo brought a letter this morning confirming Malcolm's release and requesting the pleasure of our company at the Flamingo ball.

Me: I didn't know there was a Flamingo ball.

Nell: Of course there is. It happens every year in Torquay at the Imperial Hotel. Do keep up.

Me: Sorry.

PART 4:

Autumn

CHAPTER 1:
Dave and Harriet's Cottage Pie Recipe

Nell: Today we are making David and Harriet's favourite supper of cottage pie. This recipe normally serves 10, or 7, if David is eating.

Me: Right.

Nell: You will need

- 3 tbsp. olive oil
- 11/4 kg beef mince (if you use lamb mince, it becomes a shepherd's pie)
- 2 onions, finely chopped (not recommended for dogs but fine for adults and flamingos)
- 3 carrots, chopped (give a couple of extra carrots to the dogs)
- 3 celery sticks, chopped (don't bother about giving us those)
- 2 garlic cloves, chopped (definitely not recommended for dogs)
- 1 tbsp. tomato purée
- 1 large glass of red wine (if cooking for dogs, just drink that yourself)

- 850 ml beef stock
- 4 tbsp. Worcestershire sauce (not available everywhere, and not recommended for dogs)
- a few sprigs of thyme, or a spoonful of dried thyme
- 2 bay leaves (remember to take them out along with the sprigs, please, since they're very chewy)

For the mashed potato:

- 1.8 kg potatoes chopped (Poppy favours Maris Piper, but not available everywhere)
- 22 ml milk
- 25 g butter
- 200 g strong cheddar, grated (or similar cheese)

Me: That's a lot of ingredients.

Nell: None of them are expensive, and it is a dish loved by the whole family. You can freeze any leftovers in small portions as a quick lunch.

Me: Good idea.

Nell: Don't get excited, since there is never any left over in our house.

So, Poppy has heated 1 tbsp. olive oil in a large saucepan and is frying the mince until brown. She has a very large saucepan, but if you don't have one, you can do it in batches.

Now, she is setting it aside and adding the other 2 tbsp. olive oil to the pan and frying the optional onions, carrots, and celery sticks gently for about 20 minutes until soft.

Me: It already smells lovely.

Nell: Poppy will now add the optional garlic and 1 tbsp. tomato purée and has increased the heat. She is also returning the beef to the pan.

Me: What about the red wine?

Nell: This is the time you would add the wine, but you may drink it since we don't use it for us; it will need to be boiled a little to reduce it slightly before adding the 850 ml beef stock, 4 tbsp. Worcestershire sauce, a few thyme sprigs, and the 2 bay leaves.

Me: I don't like boiled wine.

Nell: Not for drinking. If you are adding it to the beef. Good grief. Do keep up.

Poppy is bringing it all to a simmering and will let it cook uncovered for 45 minutes. The sauce should thicken during that time.

When it's cooked, remember to remove the thyme sprigs and bay leaves. David got them caught in his teeth one time.

Me: What a nuisance.

Nell: While it is cooking, Poppy is making the mashed potatoes. The 1.8 kg potatoes have been washed and chopped and are brought to the boil in cold, salted water and cooked until soft. Times vary, so keep an eye out. Approximately 30 minutes from the start.

Once it's cooked, drain well and allow to dry a little before mashing in 225 ml milk, 25 g butter and 150 g cheese. Season with salt and pepper.

Me: Can I try the mashed potato?

Nell: No. Now Poppy is spooning the meat into 2 ovenproof dishes. and spooning the mash on top. You can sprinkle the rest of the cheese on both dishes.

Me: Yummy.

Nell: Make sure your oven has been heated to 220°C / 200°C fan and cook for 25–30 minutes, until golden. Serve with cabbage and garden peas, or any vegetable of your choice.

Me: Perfect for a winter's evening.

Nell: Yes; no opening the oven to check its cooking, please. Go and sit down at the table with the others. Remember David and Harriet will be served first.

Me: Yes. Sorry.

DAVE AND HARRIET'S COTTAGE PIE RECIPE
(serves 10)

INGREDIENTS:

- 3 tbsp. / 44.4 ml olive oil
- 1¼ kg / 2 ¾ lbs. beef mince
- 2 onions
- 3 carrots, chopped
- 3 sticks of celery, chopped
- 2 garlic cloves, finely chopped
- 1 tbsp. / 14.8 ml tomato purée
- 1 large glass red wine (optional)

- 850 ml / 28.7 fl. oz. /3.6 cups beef stock
- 4 tbsp. / 59.2 ml Worcestershire sauce
- A few sprigs of thyme, or a spoonful of dried thyme
- 2 bay leaves
- 1.8 kg / 3.96 lbs. potatoes
- 225 ml / 7.6 fl. oz. / 0.95 cup milk
- 25 g / 10.9 oz. butter
- 200 g / 7.1 oz. / 0.9 cup strong cheddar, grated

METHOD:

Heat 1 tbsp. olive oil in a large saucepan and fry beef mince until browned—you may need to do this in batches. Set aside as it browns.

Put the other olive oil into the pan; add 2 finely chopped onions, 3 chopped carrots, and 3 chopped celery sticks; and cook on a gentle heat until soft, about 20 minutes.

Add 2 finely chopped garlic cloves and 1 tbsp. tomato purée, increase the heat, and cook for a few minutes, then return the beef to the pan.

Pour over a large glass of red wine, if using, and boil to reduce it slightly before adding the beef stock, Worcestershire sauce, a few thyme sprigs, and 2 bay leaves.

Bring to a simmer and cook, uncovered, for 45 minutes.

Season well, then discard the bay leaves and thyme stalks.

Meanwhile, make the mash.

In a large saucepan, cover the 1.8 kg potatoes, which you've peeled and chopped, in salted cold water, bring to the boil, and simmer until tender.

Drain well, then allow to steam dry for a few minutes.

Mash well with the milk, butter, and ¾ of the strong cheddar cheese, then season with salt and pepper.

Spoon the meat into 2 ovenproof dishes.

Pipe or spoon on the mash to cover.

Sprinkle on the remaining cheese.

If eating straight away, heat oven to 220°C / 200°C fan / gas 7 and cook for 25–30 minutes, or until the topping is golden.

Serve with green vegetables. We love garden peas.

CHAPTER 2:

Autumn Walks

Nell: It was a wonderful light on our walk yesterday.

Me: Yes, I can see.

Nell: Beautiful colours and unseasonably warm. Kev took a photo.

Me: Lovely.

Nell: Did Malcolm take care of you?

Me: Yes. Kev lit a fire, and Malcolm, Mutley, and I just relaxed together.

Nell: I think that young flamingo is going to blossom with us. He wasn't cut out for a soldier's life.

Me: I agree. Mutley was telling us about his time in the Royal Navy.

Nell: Ah yes. He saw some sights. He trained at Dartmouth, of course.

Me: I didn't know.

Nell: Well, there's a lot you don't know. Life is one big discovery, which is just as it should be.

Me: I suppose so.

Nell: Now, David has some homework from Dogs School. They wanted to know if he is still marvellous. That is his recall word, of course, resulting in a treat.

Me: Yes, he is. Extremely.

Nell: Apparently he needs to work on his anxiety.

Me: He is still afraid of the dark. Harriet always goes out with him if she can. She is fearless.

Nell: I've noticed he has taken to carrying Gladys with him in her pumpkin when he goes out at night. She uses her iBone as a light.

Me: Does she?

Nell: Yes, the effect is rather spooky, especially when David wears his tall hat and the cloak The Cat made him.

Me: So that's what it was. It all makes sense now.

Nell: What do you mean?

Me: I thought I was delirious when I looked out last night. I didn't tell you because I knew you wouldn't believe me.

Nell: Can you blame me? The fantasy world you live in.

Me: I know. Sorry.

CHAPTER 3:
Haunted Hotel, Day One

Nell: Now, are we all packed? James is here.

Me: The Cat just arrived with a huge case.

Nell: Ridiculous. We are going for just over a week.

Me: I still don't see why I can't come.

Nell: So, you think leaving Kev alone is acceptable, and who is going to run the café?

Me: But I want to stay at the Cottage Hotel too. It's my favourite place.

Nell: I will be in regular contact. You can come to the Halloween party.

Me: Have you booked your rooms?

Nell: Of course I have. They all have sea views. Mutley, David, Malcolm, and The Cat are sharing. Poppy and Harriet have a premium double with balcony, and I have a luxury room with a bay window of my own.

Me: What about Gladys?

Nell: Gladys will be in my handbag. You know that.

Me: How am I supposed to run the café on my own? It's so busy.

Nell: I've organised some members from the Whippets Institute to help. Stop fussing.

Me: I suppose I should say goodbye.

Nell: Did David just go past with Rita on a surfboard?

Me: Yes.

Nell: She either agrees to share the handbag with Gladys, or she's not coming.

Me: I wish I fitted in your handbag.

Nell: Good grief. The mere idea. See you in just over a week's time.

Me: Yes. Sorry.

CHAPTER 4:

Haunted Hotel, Day Two

Me: How is the hotel?

Nell: Lovely. Just like stepping back in time.

Me: Is your room comfortable?

Nell: Yes, it has a beautiful view of the coast. Spectacular in fact. I'm enjoying a cream tea with Malcolm and Gladys as we speak. The scones aren't up to Poppy's standard, but the clotted cream is excellent.

Me: Oh good.

Nell: "Do be careful of the jam, Gladys, dear. You know how it sticks to your fur."

Me: Have you met any of the other guests yet?

Nell: We have. There is a somewhat bohemian deaf leopard in the bar, and a rather odd sloth in the lounge. He appears to be reading the newspaper, but he hasn't moved since breakfast.

Me: Are you sure he's alive?

Nell: Oh yes. He's called Marwood.

Me: What an unusual name. How do you know?

Nell: Mutley told me. He accidentally sat on him yesterday, thinking he was a chair. He apologised, and Marwood introduced himself and said not to worry since it happens all the time.

Me: Does the leopard have a name?

Nell: It can't hear me, of course, but I believe it is called Vivian and comes from Northern Ireland. Funny name for a male leopard. It just sits there nodding and drinking whisky.

Me: What about the other guests?

Nell: They are a strange bunch, to be honest. There is a rather nervous hyena with her husband. He has something of the wolf about him. He seems to get hairier in the evenings.

Me: Oh dear.

Nell: The talk is all about ghosts and ghouls, of course. Ridiculous nonsense.

Me: It is nearly Halloween, Nell.

Nell: Oh no. That's disgusting!

Me: Has Gladys dropped the jam?

Nell: No, someone put salt in the sugar bowl. "Run down and get me some sugar, dear."

Me: You never usually call me dear.

Nell: I was talking to Malcolm, not you. You are at home. Remember? Do keep up.

Me: Yes, of course. Sorry.

Not Invited

Me: It was awfully mean of you to leave me at home when you went to the Cottage Hotel.

Nell: You go there all the time with your writer friends.

Me: Yes, but I only stay there once a year.

Nell: And am I ever invited?

Me: No. Sorry.

CHAPTER 5:
Haunted Hotel, Day Three

Nell: I've had a dreadful night.

Me: Oh no, why?

Nell: Harriet had to stay in my room because she saw a face at the window.

Me: Was someone peeking in?

Nell: She is on the second floor facing the sea.

Me: Oh dear.

Nell: It's just her age. All this talk of ghosts. It's made her nervous.

Me: Was it a dog?

Nell: A dog? Out flying across the sea at night?

Me: I thought it might be her reflection.

Nell: It was white with big black eyes.

Me: I'm getting scared now.

Nell: David is terrified. He tried to sleep under his bed and got stuck. The Cat had to call reception to help free him.

Me: Oh dear.

Nell: Then Poppy was putting her sword under her pillow and found Malcolm.

Me: Under her pillow?

Nell: Yes, he says it feels safer there.

Me: Does Poppy always put her sword under her pillow?

Nell: Of course not. Only when she is away from home.

Me: Yes, sorry.

CHAPTER 6:

Haunted Hotel, Day Four

Nell: I'm going to have a strong word with that nervous hyena and her wolfish husband.

Me: Why?

Nell: Howling all night.

Me: Are you sure it wasn't the sea?

Nell: I know the difference. Anyway, the sea doesn't laugh. Horrible cackling laughter.

Me: I hope the puppies weren't frightened.

Nell: Seeing as they were both in my room, I can assure you they were absolutely terrified.

Me: Is there enough room for you all?

Nell: Harriet is sharing my bed, and we have made a makeshift den for David with a blanket over two chairs. Fortunately, Gladys and Rita are in my handbag and Malcolm is with Poppy. She and Mutley are made of sterner stuff and are happy to stay in their rooms. Poppy has her sword, of course, and Mutley has Robert.

Me: Robert?

Nell: Robert the softly spoken Rottweiler. His bodyguard. Do keep up.

Me: Did anyone else hear the howling?

Nell: It was the talk of breakfast. Even Marwood joined in. He frowned.

Me: Why didn't anyone complain to them at breakfast?

Nell: They didn't come down. Sleeping off the madness of last night, I suspect.

Me: Probably.

Nell: Anyway, I am going to ask for their room number and knock on their door.

Me: Don't do that, Nell. It might be dangerous.

Nell: Stuff and nonsense. I can't be kept awake like this.

Me: Please be careful.

Nell: Do stop fussing. Poppy is coming with me, and she is bringing her sword.

Me: OK. Sorry.

CHAPTER 7:

Haunted Hotel, Day Five

Nell: What a dreadful cheek.

Me: Why? What's happened?

Nell: The wolf and his wife have disappeared without paying the bill.

Me: That's naughty of them.

Nell: I agree. Wolf, or werewolf, you pay your bill.

Me: Did you just say werewolf?

Nell: Yes, just another rumour. All we know is he is American and lives in London. He was last seen leaving the hotel eating a raw steak, which is odd because steak wasn't on the menu.

Me: You don't think it was the hyena he was eating, do you?

Nell: Do stop. Anyway, we have much more important things to worry about.

Me: Really? I can't imagine what.

Nell: The chef saw a face at the window last night, and now he has run off with half the kitchen staff.

Me: Oh no.

Nell: Sarah, the hotel's owner, is distraught because the hotel is fully booked. Fortunately I managed to calm her down and reminded her that we have Poppy.

Me: Poppy's not a werewolf slayer.

Nell: What are you talking about? Poppy is a chef. She is running the kitchen with Malcolm and Harriet. David, Gladys, and The Cat are waiting on tables.

Me: Goodness.

Nell: We are all doing what we can, although I draw the line at making beds.

Me: Who is the face at the window?

Nell: I don't know yet, but I mean to find out.

Me: Wear garlic. Werewolves hate it.

Nell: Stop confusing werewolves with vampires, and get a grip.

Me: Yes. Sorry.

CHAPTER 8:

Haunted Hotel, Day Six

Me: Have there been any more scares?

Nell: David set fire to a guest's feathers when he was trying to flambé a Steak Diane at the table.

Me: Feather boa?

Nell: No. Unfortunately their own. As I said to Gladys, "I know peacocks are vain creatures, but they should keep their feathers closed during dinner."

Me: Quite. Was there any howling last night?

Nell: There were strange, high-pitched voices and some clanking of chains, but nothing major. One guest claims she was followed by a dress, but that might have been due to an excess of port.

Me: A dress?

Nell: Yes. Most odd, and I'm afraid people are starting to leave. Fortunately Mutley has managed to organise a piano, so that should improve the ambience in the evenings.

Me: Yes.

Nell: David will sing and Gladys will perform a contemporary dance.

Me: Good idea.

Nell: Vivian has offered to play guitar. He is deaf, but he can still carry a tune.

Me: Like Beethoven.

Nell: No. Not a bit like Beethoven. Vivian is a Northern Irish leopard. Do keep up.

Me: Yes, sorry.

CHAPTER 9:

Haunted Hotel, Day Seven

Nell: You won't believe this.

Me: I just might.

Nell: Stephen Seagull is staying in room 103.

Me: The film star?

Nell: No, the evil head of the wicked seagull gang called the Beefies.

Me: Oh, him.

Nell: He is here with a parrot from Plymouth and one of the Pimlico pigeons.

Me: Gosh. How strange?

Nell: That's not the strange bit. Dudley saw them all with Marwood late last night.

Me: Hang on, who is Dudley?

Nell: Dudley is my friend. He lives at the hotel and is a master of disguise. Anyway, the parrot was making odd sounds.

Me: Too many fizzy drinks? It can happen.

Nell: No. Howling and clanking sounds.

Me: Oh, I see.

Nell: And Marwood was animated.

Me: How unslothlike.

Nell: Exactly. And then two small pigeons flew in to the lounge under a dress.

Me: Gosh.

Nell: And Marwood clapped his hands with glee.

Me: There is obviously more to Marwood than meets the eye.

Nell: We think Marwood may have his sights set on taking over the hotel for the Beefies. Our Marwood has his toes in a number of pies.

Me: Can't be more than three, though. He is a sloth.

Nell: This is not a joking matter.

Me: No. Sorry.

CHAPTER 10:

Haunted Hotel, Day Eight

Nell: We need you at the Cottage Hotel tomorrow at 7 p.m. precisely for the Halloween party.

Me: OK.

Nell: In fancy dress and wearing a wire.

Me: I beg your pardon.

Nell: I would suggest you come as Cousin Itt.

Me: What?

Nell: I am going as Morticia Addams, Mutley will be Gomez, and Harriet is Wednesday. Robert the Rottweiler is Uncle Fester.

Me: And Dave?

Nell: David refuses to go as Pugsley and insists on going as Zorro, with Gladys as his wife, Elena. The Cat and Rita are dancing flamenco for some reason. Vivian is joining them on guitar.

Me: What about Poppy and Malcolm?

Nell: Poppy will come as St George with Malcolm as her squire as soon as she has finished in the kitchen. She can't be expected to cook in a full suit of armour. She is lending David her sword, which I think is a grave mistake.

Me: I agree.

Nell: The plan is to ply Marwood with drink and get him to confess. We are sure he has been trying to force a sale by causing havoc.

Me: Have you told the owners?

Nell: No, it is best to keep Sarah and William in the dark for now.

Me: Where am I going to get a wire and a Cousin Itt costume?

Nell: Order them online from Ham and Scone like everyone else. Make sure it's next-day delivery.

Me: OK. Sorry.

CHAPTER 11:

Haunted Hotel, Day Nine

Me: My goodness. That was exciting. I don't think Marwood will be bothering us again anytime soon.

Nell: Neither do I.

Me: How did Dudley do that head thing? Marwood was terrified.

Nell: Yes. He soon started talking after that.

Me: When David waved his sword and Dudley's head fell off, I thought Marwood was going to faint.

Nell: Malcolm did. Fortunately, Harriet carries smelling salts.

Me: Yes. And then Dudley calmly picked his head up, tucked it under his arm, and carried on talking.

Nell: Yes. It was quite extraordinary.

Me: You never told me Dudley was a magician.

Nell: He isn't.

Me: How did he do it, then? I mean after Marwood ran off, Dudley just put his head back on, walked through the wall, and disappeared.

Nell: Yes. He bowed first, I seem to remember. He is always the gentleman.

Me: Just as if he was a real ghost.

Nell: Yes. Exactly.

Me: Wait, are you telling me that Dudley is a ghost?

Nell: I am.

Me: I've been chatting to a ghost all evening?

Nell: You have. Dudley is a very friendly ghost, though. He has lived at the Cottage Hotel for years. There was no way he was going to let Marwood, or the Beefies, take it over.

Me: Why didn't you tell us?

Nell: Dudley prefers to remain in the background. He values his privacy. Guests are honoured if they are able to make his acquaintance.

Me: Nobody would believe this if I wrote it down.

Nell: Let's see about that, shall we?

Me: Yes. Sorry.

CHAPTER 12:

Happy Halloween

Me: Happy Halloween. I hope I didn't wake you with my coffin.

Nell: What are you doing downstairs? You are not well, and what are you both wearing?

Me: Dave and I took a quick selfie.

Nell: Those aren't the hats we chose for you.

Me: Dave wanted feathers.

Nell: Good grief.

Me: Anyway, what do you say when a skeleton comes to dinner?

Nell: I don't know.

Me: Bone appetit.

Nell: That's dreadful.

Me: I knew you wouldn't find it humerus.

Nell: Have you got this out of your system now? Only I have a lot to do before the party at the café, and Harriet is waiting.

Me: Just trying to creep it real.

Nell: Poppy, Malcolm, and The Cat are already there making the final preparations.

Me: Gourd for them.

Nell: You need to be quiet.

Me: You mean don't spook unless I'm spooken to?

Nell: I'm leaving soon with David and the dancers. I expect you to be wearing your costume when we start the live link this afternoon.

Me: Yes. Let's get this party startled.

Nell: In the meantime, please get some rest. Mutley has agreed to sit with you for a while. I really have to go.

Me: Don't forget to bring me back some cake and a sand witch.

Nell: Enough. Back to bed, right now.

Me: Yes. Sorry.

PART 5:

Winter

CHAPTER 1:
Mutley's Yorkshire Pudding Recipe

Nell: Today we are making Mutley's favourite Yorkshire puddings to go with our roast beef.

Me: They are very British, aren't they?

Nell: Yes; once tried, never forgotten. They are a little like a savoury pancake, I suppose, and definitely need to be eaten with gravy.

Me: They go with any kind of roasted meat. Poppy always serves them with our Sunday roast, but some people have them with sausages and onion gravy.

Nell: Yes.

The ingredients are

- 140 g / 200 ml / 4.9 oz. US plain flour

- 4 eggs

- 200 ml / 7 oz. / 0.4 pints milk

- Sunflower oil

- Salt and pepper to season

Me: Do you just mix it all together?

Nell: Certainly not. Poppy begins by heating the oven to 230°C / 210°C fan, or 450°F / 400°F fan and then drizzling a little sunflower oil into 2 4-hole Yorkshire pudding tins, or you can use a 12-hole nonstick muffin tin.

Me: You get 12 with the second one instead of 8.

Nell: Yes, but they are smaller. Poppy is now placing the tins in the oven to heat through.

While this is happening, you can make the batter.

Me: How exciting.

Nell: Tip 140 g plain flour into a bowl, and beat in 4 eggs until smooth.

Me: OK.

Nell: Now gradually add 200 ml milk and keep on beating until the mixture is completely smooth and lump free.

Nell: Poppy will season it with salt and pepper and is now pouring the batter into a jug. She is about to remove the hot tins from the oven, so stand back.

Me: It's smoking hot.

Nell: Yes. It is meant to be. Watch how carefully and evenly Poppy is pouring the batter into the holes.

Me: Yes.

Nell: Once filled, the tins go back into the oven for 20–25 minutes until the Yorkshire puddings have risen and turned a golden brown. No opening the door to check on them.

Me: When they are ready, they have to be eaten immediately, don't they?

Nell: They do, so you need to make sure your roast beef and gravy are ready. Poppy has it all under control. Only Mutley is allowed a Yorkshire pudding in the paw. No stealing.

Me: Yes. Sorry.

MUTLEY'S YORKSHIRE PUDDING RECIPE

INGREDIENTS:

- 140 g / 4.9 oz. / 0.61 cup plain flour
- 4 eggs
- 200 ml / 6.8 fl. oz. / 0.85 cup milk
- sunflower oil for cooking

METHOD:

Heat oven to 230°C / 210°C fan.

Drizzle a little sunflower oil evenly into 2 4-hole Yorkshire pudding tins, or a 12-hole nonstick muffin tin, and place in the oven to heat through.

To make the batter, tip 140 g plain flour into a bowl and carefully beat in 4 eggs until smooth.

Gradually add milk and carry on beating until the mix is smooth.

Season with salt and pepper.

Pour the batter into a jug, then remove the hot tins from the oven.

Carefully and evenly pour the batter into the holes.

Place the tins back in the oven and leave undisturbed for 20–25 minutes until the puddings have puffed up and browned.

Serve immediately, preferably with roast beef, vegetables, and gravy.

CHAPTER 2:

We Love the Beach Whatever the Weather

Nell: Well, that was invigorating.

Me: Yes. Walking by the sea is good for the soul. As you always say, "In rain, or shine, the beach is fine. I think about it all the time."

Nell: I most certainly do not. Stop getting carried away and putting words in my mouth.

Me: But you do love it.

Nell: I do. It always blows away the cobwebs, and if you follow your walk with a fish finger sandwich, or a sizzling sausage at the Beachhouse in South Milton, then all the better.

Me: Did you have to inspect the kitchen though, Nell?

Nell: I like to check everything is up to standard.

Me: You like to check on the sausages, you mean.

Nell: Jonathan and I enjoyed them enormously. I ate a little of your fish, but it didn't have the piquancy of our dish.

Me: Yes. Jonathan does enjoy tomato ketchup. After all that running, you certainly deserved a good lunch.

Nell: Alice's ball-throwing skills are not up to Kev's, but still very acceptable.

Me: What about mine?

Nell: Shall we just gloss over yours? Remember the throwing-the-Wellington-boot incident?

Me: It wasn't my finest hour.

Nell: You hit yourself on the head.

Me: I didn't know it would go backwards.

Nell: Let's leave the throwing to Kev and Alice, shall we? She may not throw far, but at least the ball goes in the right direction.

Me: Yes. Sorry.

CHAPTER 3:

Happy First Advent

Nell: Jonathan and the team have made an excellent job of the tree.

Me: Yes, it's beautiful.

Nell: David fell asleep halfway through, but it has been an exciting time for him with his new responsibilities.

Me: I think you were right to make him events coordinator.

Nell: Yes. Everyone needs responsibility. Gladys will be his right-paw dog. They work well together. It also means he can join in everything. A busy pup is a happy pup.

Me: It was kind of The Cat to allow Jonathan onto the decorating team.

Nell: He has style and he knows what he likes. The Cat spotted it immediately. Harriet is his teammate since she is excellent at craftwork and is a good listener.

Me: Is Mutley involved too?

Nell: Yes, Mutley is overseeing proceedings. He likes to call it Keeping an Eye on Things. It carries a great deal of responsibility but can be done from the sofa and involves regular naps.

Me: Sounds like my kind of job.

Nell: Now, it's First Advent Sunday today, so David will be singing and a candle must be lit.

Me: Yes, the Advent wreath is ready.

Nell: Good. Poppy and Malcolm are cooking a full Christmas dinner of turkey with all the trimmings.

Me: How lovely.

Nell: We can't have Jonathan and Alice missing out, since they have to go back to Berlin before Christmas, so we are having an extra Christmas with games after dinner. Your little sister Alexandra is invited too.

Me: Perfect.

Nell: Malcolm is serving prawn cocktail for lunch, and there will be ice cream for those who want it.

Me: You can never have enough ice cream.

Nell: I think you and I both know that is not true. I think one ice cream each will be plenty.

Me: You are right. Sorry.

CHAPTER 4:

What Makes a Good Listener?

Nell: Chris is an excellent listener. It's a shame he lives so far away in Toronto.

Me: What makes a good listener?

Nell: Good question. David isn't much of a listener. He's too impatient. He gets up and walks away while you are still talking.

Me: I know what you mean. We all need to be heard.

Nell: Harriet is very good at listening, but sometimes she needs to confide, and Chris knows that.

Me: Yes. It's knowing when to listen.

Nell: Gladys is a surprisingly good listener.

Me: Is she?

Nell: Yes. We often go out together now. Sometimes by accident, to be honest, since I don't always realise she is in my handbag.

Me: Yes.

Nell: Yesterday, for instance, we were in Waterbones looking at books when a portly corgi in a Balmoral bonnet said to her friend, "That lab is talking to its handbag."

Me: How rude?

Nell: Well, I wasn't having it. I strolled over and said, "Excuse me, madam, but I think you will find I am talking to a black Pomeranian. Not that it is any of your business."

Me: What did the corgi say?

Nell: She turned on her paws and left.

Me: Poppy is rubbish at listening.

Nell: Poppy is too busy to listen. She has her paws in far too many pies.

Me: Mutley likes to listen.

Nell: Mutley is deaf. He can't hear a word you are saying, so he usually just nods to keep you happy.

Me: You don't always listen.

Nell: I think a pot of Earl Grey is needed.

Me: You have selective hearing. You know you do.

Nell: And a few biscuits.

Me: You hear only what suits you.

Nell: Digestive biscuit, or shortbread?

Me: Shortbread.

Nell: Good choice.

Me: You see—you heard me then.

Nell: You are a good listener.

Me: Thank you.

Nell: The only problem is you tend to write things down.

Me: I know I do.

Nell: And then you share it with everybody. So some things are safer shared with Gladys, if you know what I mean.

Me: You're right. Sorry.

CHAPTER 5:

It's Christmas Eve

Me: Happy Christmas Eve, everyone. What a great photo of you all on the beach. Where's Mutley?

Nell: He was back at the Gastrobus having a cheeky mulled wine with Ernest.

Me: Do I know Ernest?

Nell: Probably not. Elderly Jack Russell, spectacles, smokes a pipe?

Me: No. Doesn't ring a bell.

Nell: Now we are performing the Nativity at 6 p.m., so please make sure you take your seat in good time.

Me: Are you playing Mary?

Nell: Of course not. I am the narrator. Harriet is Mary and Jim is Joseph.

Me: Lovely.

Nell: David, Malcolm, and The Cat are the Three Kings in crowns and sequinned cloaks.

Me: I didn't imagine Malcolm as a king.

Nell: He wanted to be a shepherd, but the farm dogs had already been cast.

Me: And Poppy?

Nell: She's the innkeeper, and to be honest, her performance is a little too forceful for my liking. I don't think a sword is necessary.

Me: Is Gladys in it?

Nell: She wanted to be the Baby Jesus in my handbag, but when we explained he can't do a contemporary dance she opted for Herod.

Me: Who is Jesus then?

Nell: The Cat's Chihuahua. It's small and well behaved.

Me: You've forgotten Mutley.

Nell: Of course we haven't forgotten Mutley. He is the Archangel Gabriel. I'm not sure about flying him in, but he says he will be fine.

Me: I hope so.

Nell: Ron Gilbert, the Great Dane, is stage managing with John the Doberman assisting, so we are in safe paws.

Me: It's going to be a lovely Christmas, isn't it?

Nell: Yes, it is.

Me: We shall be thinking of those we love both near and far. Even if they can't be with us, they are here in our hearts.

Nell: Yes. Always. Now get your coat on; there's a turkey waiting to be collected.

Me: At the butcher's?

Nell: No, at the station. He's called Timothy, and he needs a safe place for a few days.

Me: Of course. Sorry.

CHAPTER 6:

Happy Christmas

Nell: We have a busy day ahead of us.

Me: Yes. Where is Timothy the Turkey, by the way?

Nell: Poppy gave up her den with the soft cushion so he had somewhere quiet and warm to sleep. The poor thing was exhausted. It's been a tough few months.

Me: Yes, I can imagine. What about yesterday evening, though? Quite the surprise.

Nell: If you mean Mutley doing a somersault midflight, then I won't disagree. I think Ron Gilbert was a little overconfident with the flying ropes.

Me: Yes, it was a bit worrying.

Nell: Fortunately, David was tall enough to untangle his wings and rescue his halo.

Me: But when his dress fell over his eyes, it must have been quite frightening.

Nell: It wasn't a dress. It was the archangel's robe. Anyway, Mutley took it all in his stride and even took a bow once he was back on the ground.

Me: I meant our surprise guests, actually. When I heard that deep voice singing, I knew it was Charlie.

Nell: Yes. He and David's love, Sally the Golden Retriever, made quite an entrance dressed as Father Christmas and his beautiful reindeer.

Me: Dave jumped off the stage and whirled Sally around.

Nell: Yes. Charlie and I were more dignified.

Me: I saw you smooching, Nell. It was very romantic.

Nell: I must say I wasn't expecting Michael Bouvier. I mean, I know he is everywhere at Christmas, but it was very kind of him to come and sing for us.

Me: Yes. Gladys and Count Bingo Flamingo can certainly move.

Nell: I think she should have removed her beard. I know she was playing Herod, but it was too much.

Me: Happy Christmas, darling Nell.

Nell: Happy Christmas, my dear. Enough sentimentality; we need a cup of Earl Grey and a couple of scones, or we will never get through the day.

Me: Yes. Sorry.

CHAPTER 7:

Happy New Year

Me: Nell and I would like to wish you all a very Happy New Year.

Nell: That's a great action photo of Harriet and me. You definitely didn't take it.

Me: No, I didn't, Nell. Thank you for that. It was our friend Marian.

Nell: Lovely lady. Lovely photos.

Me: I agree.

Nell: It was quite a party yesterday.

Me: Yes. I've never seen so many flamingos.

Nell: Gladys thinks that's why Malcolm and Timothy won the dance competition. Did you hear the applause? Personally I thought their fandango was a sight to behold, and the win was thoroughly deserved.

Me: Timothy's feather boa was inspired. Nothing can beat Poppy's pasa doble, to be honest.

Nell: No. She is in a league of her own. I feel John might have been better as the bullfighter than the cape, though. He is a Doberman after all, and Poppy is a small terrier.

Me: True. Has Charlie gone?

Nell: Yes. He and Sally had to get back to London. Some crisis brewing.

Me: I think this is going to be our year, Nell.

Nell: Yes. An important year. The birth of a new grandchild in May, your book, and you turn 60 at the end of this month, and Kev in August.

Me: Don't remind me of that.

Nell: Life goes on, and we shall embrace it with all four paws.

Me: I don't have four paws.

Nell: But I do, and that's enough paws for the both of us.

Me: Yes, it is. Sorry.

CHAPTER 8:

David Wants to Join the Crew

Me: Look at Dave and Tony the postman. They are so sweet together.

Nell: Yes. Although The Cat is a little annoyed.

Me: Jealousy?

Nell: Not entirely. David was in the middle of a fitting for a winter waistcoat when he heard Tony's van arrive.

Me: Oh dear.

Nell: So he just leapt up and rushed out to greet him. There were sequins everywhere.

Me: I'm not sure sequins belong on a winter waistcoat.

Nell: We are talking about The Cat here. Gladys has sequins on her bathing cap.

Me: I didn't know she wore one.

Nell: It's a ridiculous thing, but The Cat says it makes Gladys look more streamlined when she's wearing her wetsuit.

Me: Was The Cat very angry with Dave?

Nell: You know David. No one can ever be angry with him for long.

Me: I know. When he gives you that sad little look, you just can't stay cross.

Nell: Ah yes. David is the master of the "I'm awfully sorry—I don't know how it happened" look.

Me: He is.

Nell: Harriet has more of a wide-eyed, innocent "Who me?" look.

Me: Yes.

Nell: By the way, David wants to audition for Tony's sea shanty crew.

Me: The "Old Gaffers"?

Nell: Don't be so rude.

Me: No. That's their name. They perform all over the place. They even have a Facebook page.

Nell: Anyway, David seems to think he would fit in perfectly. I hope Tony lets him down gently.

Me: You never know, Nell.

Nell: First, David is not even remotely old. Second, he is a Labrador.

Me: He could be their salty sea dog.

Nell: Good grief.

Me: I can see him now in navy blue with a little sequinned hat on his head, singing his heart out. People would love it.

Nell: Just stop. You are getting carried away again.

Me: Yes. Sorry.

CHAPTER 9:

Dealing with Disappointment

Me: I'm ever so worried about Dave.

Nell: Leave him be. He is Dealing with Disappointment. A valuable life skill.

Me: So, Tony never came?

Nell: No. David waited a long time, but we think Tony may have gone on his winter break.

Me: Poor darling Dave.

Nell: He is very low, but he is being brave and Harriet is consoling him.

Me: Bless her.

Nell: Anyway, David has earned extra points for excellent Waiting Skills yesterday, and his report card is looking a lot better.

Me: He has a report card?

Nell: Of course. Both he and Harriet have had one since they started training.

Me: Did you tell him Tony will be back next week?

Nell: I did, and we agreed that he can meet him at the gate, and a little jumping is allowed due to the length of separation.

Me: He still looks very low.

Nell: It's nothing that some good sea air and a swim won't solve. As I explained to both David and Harriet, a Labrador has to learn many things, and Dealing with Disappointment is one of the hardest.

Me: Yes.

Nell: I myself am constantly disappointed by you, for instance.

Me: Well, that's not very nice. I'm sure Kev disappoints you too.

Nell: Maybe. But I can't think of anything he has done right now.

Me: Typical. I've probably got a report card I don't know about.

Nell: You have.

Me: Seriously? Can I see it?

Nell: You cannot.

Me: That's not fair.

Nell: Deal with the Disappointment.

Me: Yes. Sorry.

I'm Rather Proud of Us

Me: We make a good team, don't we?

Nell: Yes. I am actually rather proud of us, even if you are exasperating at times.

Me: You mean the world to me.

Nell: Likewise. You and me. Always. You know that.

Me: Yes. Sorry.

CHAPTER 10:

Shenanigans

Me: What is going on?

Nell: We decided to have a game of Shenanigans with Kev, and, as usual, David took it too far.

Me: What is Shenanigans? It looks fun.

Nell: It's a Labrador game. We all play it.

Me: How does it work?

Nell: You take it in turns. It involves a lot of movement and weaving in and out. Someone is "It" and then passes it on.

Me: You've never played it with me.

Nell: We play it with you all the time.

Me: I didn't know.

Nell: Yes, that's half the fun.

Me: Does Kev know?

Nell: Of course, he does. He is an excellent player.

Me: Why didn't you tell me?

Nell: You are at your best when you don't know. Less worried.

Me: Could we play now?

Nell: No, we are exhausted.

Me: Please, Nell. I want to play.

Nell: Patience is a virtue; we labs know this is true. Often found in dogs, but seldom found in you.

Me: Well, that's not true.

Nell: You won't mind waiting then.

Me: Yes. Sorry.

CHAPTER 11:

Whatever

Me: I know you aren't in the best of moods.

Nell: I am not.

Me: But I had to take you to see Alex the vet yesterday.

Nell: Whatever.

Me: You needed your ear drops.

Nell: I didn't need the shame of a public weigh-in.

Me: The scales are in reception.

Nell: I didn't need my weight discussed by all and sundry. Including a rather large Pyrenean mountain dog who had no business getting involved.

Me: I agree. The nurse thought you looked a little slimmer.

Nell: Do you know what it's like to have David being marvellous all the time and showered with treats, and Harriet eating like a horse and staying slim and petite?

Me: I sort of do know, Nell, since my sisters could always eat what they liked and I never could.

Nell: I am who I am.

Me: I know, and I wouldn't change anything about you. We all love you, Nell. Would you like a pot of Earl Grey by the fire?

Nell: That would be kind. And a soft blanket, perhaps?

Me: Of course. I'll ask Harriet to bring you the latest *Good Housekeeping*.

Nell: And just a few of Poppy's shortbread biscuits?

Me: You are not supposed to have those.

Nell: I understand. Shortbread is reserved for the young and marvellous.

Me: I can offer you a carrot.

Nell: I wouldn't if I were you.

Me: No. Sorry.

CHAPTER 12:

Strategic Placement

Nell: What is it now?

Me: There is no need to snap at me.

Nell: Today is exceptionally busy, since the puppies are sitting their mock exams later and we still have some revising to do.

Me: I just wanted to discuss you getting in the way.

Nell: Getting in whose way?

Me: Getting in everyone's way. Why do you have to do that?

Nell: Are you talking about Strategic Placement?

Me: I might be. You know the way you and the puppies always lie in difficult places, so we have to keep stepping over you, or walking round you?

Nell: Yes, clever isn't it?

Me: No. It's ever so annoying.

Nell: Strategic Placement is one of the first skills a young Labrador learns. One stretches out to full length, keeping a close eye on all comings and goings. Correct Placement is, of course, essential. If food is being prepared, the distance is reduced.

Me: But you are in the way.

Nell: No. We are involved. Whether you are cooking or going to the bathroom, we are placed strategically to offer maximum support.

Me: I don't find it supportive. I keep telling you to get out of the way.

Nell: But answer this. Do you miss us when we aren't there?

Me: That's not fair. You know I like to have you with me.

Nell: Give me an honest answer. Do you find yourself actually wishing we were there because it's part of your daily life and even comforting?

Me: Well, yes. Sort of.

Nell: I rest my case. Now leave the examination room, since we have a lot to get through.

Me: Ok. Sorry.

CHAPTER 13:

Surf Chasing

Me: And they're off. Surf Chasing.

Nell: Good grief.

Me: Surf Dude Dave is in the lead. Ears flapping and paws thundering as he charges through the sea.

Nell: Surf Dude Dave?

Me: Closely followed on his left by amazing Surf Sister Harriet, swift of paw and built for speed.

Nell: Surf Sister Harriet? Have you been drinking?

Me: Bringing up the rear to his right and poised for the kill is Surf Queen Nell.

Nell: I beg your pardon. Bringing up the rear? There is no rear about this.

Me: Well, you are at the back.

Nell: Harriet and I are on a par. It's the angle. Anyway, I got the ball.

Me: Yes. You are the Surf Queen.

Nell: My Retrieving Skills are unparalleled.

Me: Although, to be fair, Dave ran right past the ball and kept going, and Harriet usually lets you have it.

Nell: That's rich coming from someone who has trouble throwing a ball.

Me: Yes, sorry.

CHAPTER 14:

The Beast from the East

Me: What are you all doing?

Nell: Waiting for the Beast.

Me: Are you waiting for Dave, then?

Nell: No, not David. Don't be silly.

Me: Oh, you mean the Beast from the East?

Nell: I do.

Me: Bit scary.

Nell: It's just snow and cold winds. That's all.

Me: What if we run out of supplies?

Nell: Unlikely.

Me: Or the power is cut?

Nell: We have candles and logs for the wood burner.

Me: I will have to cuddle you for warmth, Nell.

Nell: You certainly will not. I need my space.

Me: How will I survive?

Nell: Actually, this is where David will triumph.

Me: Of course, Dave loves cuddles.

Nell: He does.

Me: I'll just cuddle Dave all day.

Nell: I think you will have to share him.

Me: Dave loves me.

Nell: Yes, but he also loves Kev and Harriet, not to mention Poppy, Mutley, Gladys, Malcolm, The Cat, and Timothy the Turkey.

Me: True.

Nell: Fortunately, there is a lot of David to go around, so I'm sure he will be over to warm you up very soon.

Me: I hope so.

Nell: David isn't the only one who cares you know. How about a cup of Earl Grey and one of Poppy's scones by the fire? Mutley is going to play some winter songs on the piano. We shall all sing, and Gladys will be performing a contemporary dance.

Me: Yes, please. Sorry.

❧ GLOSSARY ❧

The Artful Dodger: In Charles Dickens' novel Oliver Twist Oliver is kidnapped by an evil moneylender called Fagin and forced to work as a pickpocket with a gang of boys led by the Artful Dodger.

Balmoral bonnet: A traditional Scottish hat.

Bank holiday: In the UK, when banks are officially closed. Usually a public holiday.

Barcelona: A very powerful and dramatic song by the late Freddie Mercury of Queen and the operatic singer Montserrat Caballe.

Bounder: Old-fashioned word for a dishonourable man.

The Campaign: A cause started by Nell to keep the beaches open to dogs all year round. In the UK, many beaches are closed to dogs from May until October.

"...the cheek of it...": An exclamation of shocked disapproval at something someone has said, or done. It means, "How dare he?"

Cowes Week: One of the oldest sailing regattas in the world. It started in 1826 and is held every August in the Solent off the small town of Cowes, on the Isle of Wight, UK.

Fagin: See The Artful Dodger.

Frenchies: Slang term for French bulldogs.

Hercule Poirot: Agatha Christie's famous detective.

"It's not on": Means something is not OK; something is not right.

Jam roly poly: A traditional British dessert usually served with custard.

Je ne regretted rien: A famous song by the French singer Edith Piaf. Translated, it means, "No, I do not regret anything."

Jo le taxi: A popular French song from 1987, sung by Vanessa Paradis, who used to be married to American actor, Johnny Depp.

❧ GLOSSARY ❧

Miss Moneypenny: The secretary to M, the head of the Secret Intelligence Service known as MI6, in the James Bond franchise.

Poldark: A TV series set in the southernmost county of the UK called Cornwall which is right next to Devon. The main characters are Ross and Demelza and there is a lot of riding along the cliffs by the sea with the wind in their hair.

Radio Devon: A local BBC radio station.

Saturday Kitchen: A Saturday morning TV cooking programme on the BBC.

Squiffy: Slightly drunk.

St. George: Saint George is the patron saint of England. St. George's Day is usually celebrated on 23rd April. He is the patron saint of England. The legend of St. George and the Dragon describes the real-life St. George taming and slaying a dragon that demanded human sacrifices. Saint George rescues the princess who was chosen as the next offering.

Stilton: A famous, English blue cheese.

Torquay Operatic Society: An amateur musical theatre society based in the town of Torquay. (See the map on p. 16.)

Truro: The only city in Cornwall, the most southerly county in the UK, next to Devon.

Waterstones: A large chain of bookstores in the UK.

Weetabix: A breakfast cereal

❧ A NOTE TO YOU, DEAR READER ❦

Nell: That's a photo of me with Alice.

Me: I know it's my favourite. I love your dear faces.

Nell: I know you do. Now, you need to talk to our readers.

Me: Yes, if you have enjoyed reading this and would like to read more...

Nell: What do you mean if?

Me: Well, that's what you say, isn't it?

Nell: Certainly not. If they've got this far they must be enjoying themselves.

Me: Anyway, if you would like to read more please go to our website.

Nell: www.conversationswithnell.org

Me: Or follow our daily blog on Facebook.

Nell: Just search for Conversations with Nell and you will find our page.

Me: We are on Instagram too.

Nell: Yes.

Me: We would love you to join us so please keep in touch.

Nell: It would be most gratifying.

Me: Thank you so much for buying this book.

Nell: And don't worry there will be more.

Me: Will there?

Nell: Of course. We are never going to run out of conversations.

Me: You are right. Sorry.

ABOUT SARA MARTIN

Me: I've always talked to my animals. I used to make up stories all the time.

Nell: You wrote your first play when you were 7.

Me: Words are my life.

Nell: You lived in Africa for 6 years broadcasting for BBC World Service and teaching drama to teenagers.

Me: I also worked as a subtitler and editor in Berlin, and I speak fluent German.

Nell: You have an MA in English language and literature and you're also a professional voiceover artist.

Me: But my dream has always been to write.

Nell: It's why we moved down to Devon.

Me: Yes, I am living the dream.

Nell: I may just be a Labrador, but I feel I played a part in all this.

Me: Yes. Sorry.